THE EDUCATION OF
MISS PATTERSON

For young Miss Patricia Patterson, life seemed a dream—until her guardian, Lord Charles Gaunt, cast a shadow over her days of idleness and enchanting evenings of dazzling balls and delicious flirtations.

Lord Charles demanded she act the part of a proper and perfectly boring young Miss. Even worse, he insisted she devote her waking hours to cultivating her mind rather than captivating her swarm of admirers.

Thus the battle was joined—between the handsome, arrogant aristocrat who had Patricia in his lawful power...and Patricia, who vowed to turn this hateful tyrant into her lovelorn slave...

THE EDUCATION OF
MISS PATTERSON

The Education of Miss Patterson

by
Marion Chesney

Magna Large Print Books
Long Preston, North Yorkshire,
England.

British Library Cataloguing in Publication Data.

Chesney, Marion
   The education of Miss Patterson.

  A catalogue record for this book is
  available from the British Library

  ISBN 0-7505-0155-3

First published in Great Britain by Severn House Publishers
Ltd., 1992

Published in Large Print 1992 by arrangement with Severn
House Publishers Ltd.

Printed and bound in Great Britain by
T.J. Press (Padstow) Ltd., Cornwall, PL28 8RW.

For Harry and Charlie
With love

ONE

'What do you think, Simpers?'

Miss Patricia Patterson held up the silk purse she had just netted.

Her governess, Miss Simpkin, smiled indulgently. 'Beautiful. Quite beautiful, Miss Patricia. You are so clever. I declare I have never met a young lady who could do so much. Is that not true, Miss Evans?'

Patricia's old nanny, who had been dozing in a rocker by the nursery fire, came awake with a start and said automatically, 'Prettiest girl for miles around is my little miss. None to touch her,' and fell asleep again.

The nursery fire crackled cheerfully, and well-trimmed oil lamps cast a rosy glow over the small room.

Patricia was sixteen years of age and could have used any of the magnificent rooms downstairs, but she much preferred the shabby comfort of the old nursery, not to mention the doting compliments from her old nanny and governess.

She was a pretty girl, rather on the plump side. Her hair, a true strawberry blonde, was her greatest beauty, but she also had wide, pansy-brown eyes, a small straight nose, and a perfect mouth.

Although her parents had died the year before, Patricia considered herself the luckiest of girls.

Her parents had been elderly—her birth coming as a great surprise to her mother when the late Mrs Patterson had found herself with child at the great age of forty. She had not seen much of them, but when she did they had always praised and petted her and told her she was wonderful. They had both died in an influenza epidemic and although, for a while, she had felt their loss keenly, that loss was quickly healed by her ever-present companions, Miss Simpkin and Miss Evans.

Miss Simpkin had never really exerted herself to teach Patricia very much, and since Patricia detested lessons, they both got along very well. Patricia adored all kinds of gossip and frivolity and Gothic novels.

A certain Lord Charles Gaunt had been appointed her guardian in her father's will.

Patricia had never met Lord Charles, but her father had often spoken of him, praising him as a young man of remarkable good sense. Patricia thought he was probably a bore.

So far, Lord Charles had not put in an appearance. He was to have control of Patricia's home, Burnham House, its estates, and Patricia's fortune until she married.

He had written from time to time from the Continent, brief notes apologizing for business affairs which were preventing him from returning.

As the weeks passed, Lord Charles's letters stopped. Patricia had high hopes they would never be troubled with him. She did not need anyone to find her a husband. There were men a-plenty in the county, and lots of delicious parties and balls to attend.

She knew some of the old dowagers at the last hunt ball had complained to Miss Simpkin, who had acted as chaperone, that she was flirting too boldly and behaving in a disgustingly *fast* manner, but Miss Simpkin could find no fault in her beloved Patricia.

The house was excellently run by a

well-trained staff, and the estates by a competent steward; all Patricia had to do was to amuse herself and talk about beaux, and send to London for expensive gowns to wear at the next county ball or party.

'Thank goodness the weather is so bad,' yawned Patricia. 'I do not feel like entertaining anyone and I do not think callers will venture out in such weather.'

The wind howled around the eaves and the rain pattered against the glass of the windows, emphasizing the coziness of the room.

Then there came the rumble of carriage wheels below.

'Oh, fiddle! Callers.' Patricia ran to the window and looked down.

'Well, there is a very grand coachman on the box,' she said. 'Dressed in the finest stare. So many capes and the latest in beaver hats. Outriders with flambeaux. They must have come a long way, whoever they are. I can only see the tops of their heads. No, the driver must be some fine lord, driving the carriage himself, for what is recognizable as a coachman has appeared around the other side of the carriage.

'Good heavens! What a quantity of luggage ...' Her voice trailed away and she swung about, wide-eyed. 'Never say Lord Charles has arrived at last.'

Miss Simpkin joined her at the window. In the flickering light of the torches, she could see a tall figure striding about giving orders.

'I think it must be,' she twittered. 'Run and put on your *best* muslin, Miss Patricia.'

Patricia did not have a lady's maid, being content to call on the help of one of the chambermaids if she needed her hair frizzled, or the tapes of her gown tied at the back. Her, hair that evening was done up in curl papers, since she had been trying out the new style called *à la Brutus,* which involved normal-sized curls on the front and masses of tight curls over the rest of the head. One was supposed to leave in the papers for at least twenty-four hours to ensure the correct effect. Most gentlewomen sat down to dinner these days in their curl papers if there was to be a ball or party the following night.

She reluctantly took them out. An hour later she was still not satisfied with the effect.

The visitor *was* Lord Charles, and an increasingly nervous butler had sent up two messages already to say that his lordship was waiting to speak to Patricia in the drawing room.

Each time, Patricia had crossly replied he would just have to wait. Hair was more important.

It took her another hour before she was satisfied with her appearance. She descended the stairs with Miss Simpkin twittering in her wake.

Most of the house was pretty much the way Patricia's parents had left it, a mixture of old and new furniture, statuary brought back from the Grand Tour, and the late Mrs Patterson's collection of china.

But Patricia had refurbished the drawing room to her own taste. Sofas and armchairs were upholstered in pink and gold. Several bad portraits of Patricia painted by local amateurs graced the walls. Huge bunches of exotic flowers from the hothouses—arranged every day whether or not there were guests—scented the air. A large fire burned on the hearth.

Looking very out of place in the middle of all this flowery feminine pink and gold was Lord Charles. He was a very tall, handsome man in a harsh-featured way. His thick hair was artistically dressed, but worn longer than was the current fashion and curled on his collar. He was wearing a severe black coat with silver buttons, buff knee breeches, and clocked stockings. His white cravat was a snowy miracle of intricate folding and starch. His eyes were heavy-lidded and very green—a disconcerting emerald green without a trace of hazel.

Patricia waited confidently for his eyes to light up with pleasure when he saw her. But he glared at her and did not bother to walk forward to greet her. He merely stood where he was in front of the fire.

'I am glad you have decided to honour me with your company, Miss Patricia,' he said. 'Did your parents never tell you it is rude to keep guests waiting?'

'I did not expect you, my lord,' said Patricia. 'I wished to look my best for you and so I took time over my appearance.'

She pirouetted in front of him, giggled, and sank into a curtsy.

The green eyes surveying her looked, if anything, a trifle colder and harder.

'Sit down!' He pulled forward a chair. 'Who is this lady?'

'My governess, Simpers.'

'For God's sake!'

'I m-mean, Miss Simpkin,' stammered Patricia, beginning to feel very nervous. Not one gentleman in all her young life had failed to be charmed by her.

Lord Charles bowed to Miss Simpkin and said, 'Please leave me alone with my ward, Miss Simpkin. I shall speak to you presently.'

Miss Simpkin felt she should say something complimentary about her charge, but the tall autocrat in front of her frightened her to death. She emitted various rabbity squeaks, such as 'Too kind...honoured...dear Miss Patricia...' and fled the room.

'Good,' said Lord Charles, flicking out the tails of his coat and sitting down. 'Now, Patricia, I am sorry I took so long to get here, but business affairs kept me abroad. Who has been taking care of you since the sad death of your parents?'

'I do not need anyone to take care of me,' said Patricia, trying to copy his haughty manner and failing miserably. 'I have my governess and my old nanny for company. The house, as you see, is well run and the servants excellent. I have a good steward to oversee the land.'

'Do you have friends? It must be a very

quiet and boring life for you.'

'Oh, *no.*' Patricia brightened. 'There are so many balls and parties, particularly in the winter. Why, there is at least one a week.'

His thin brows snapped together.

'You are too young to go to balls or parties. You should not even have your hair up—if "up" can describe that shorn-sheep look of yours.'

'You are sadly out of the World,' said Patricia. 'This coiffure is called *à la Brutus* and is all the crack.'

'I am well aware of the current fashions. If you must wear these outlandish styles, then employ a hairdresser and do not attempt to arrange it yourself.'

'I *did* employ a hairdresser.'

'Liar.' He smiled, and Patricia felt quite dizzy.

'I am glad to see you still have a governess,' he went on. 'Education is very important. May I see your books?'

'Of course. There are some on the table beside you.'

Lord Charles quirked an eyebrow at the pile of Gothic horror stories and said, 'I mean, your schoolbooks. What have you been studying? Geometry? Italian?'

17

'No, *stoopid!*' laughed Patricia. 'Ladies do not need to learn any of that nonsense, as well you know. I can knit and sew to perfection. I can paint watercolours and play the pianoforte. What more could possibly be required of me?'

'I feel that, were your brain disciplined, it might improve your pert manner. I am sorry to say there is a certain sad vulgarity about your behaviour, Patricia, not to mention your taste.'

His eyes raked over her, from the low cut of her pink and gold gown, with its multitude of bows and frills, to silk flowers in her hair.

'Oh!' Patricia gasped with outrage.

'But that can be mended. You are still very young. I shall find a lady to instruct you. Miss Simpkin is obviously not up to the task of disciplining a hoyden such as you.'

'I have never been so insulted in all my life!'

'Then it is time you were. When do we dine?'

Patricia stared at him in a fury. He talked calmly of getting rid of poor Simpers, of disciplining *her*, he had grossly insulted her, and now he was calmly demanding food.

She was *not* vulgar. She was *not* a hoyden.

'I usually dine in the nursery with Miss Simpkin and Nanny Evans,' said Patricia. 'That is, unless I have guests.'

'You have a guest now.' He rang the bell and asked the butler. 'When is dinner to be served?'

'We were only awaiting your call, my lord,' said the butler with what Patricia thought was cringing obsequiousness.

'Then we shall dine immediately. Your arm, Miss Patricia.'

Patricia, her head held high, stalked in front of him. He caught her arm and pulled her back. 'Do not disgrace yourself in front of the servants,' he muttered. And then, tucking her arm under his own, he led her to the dining room.

Since there was only the two of them, the dining table had been shortened, but there was still a long distance between them when they sat down at opposite ends.

A footman carried in a tureen of mulligatawny soup and placed it in front of Lord Charles. The butler poured a glass of Rhenish for Lord Charles and moved down the table to fill Patricia's glass.

'No,' said Lord Charles gently. 'Lemonade, I think.'

'I am accustomed to wine,' said Patricia crossly.

'I have no doubt. But while I am your guardian, you will confine yourself to fruit cup and lemonade until your first Season.'

A formal dinner normally lasted for five hours, but since this family dinner was regarded as semiformal, Patricia could hope to escape after only two hours. She was so furious, she mumbled short replies to his questions and barely touched her food. The soup was followed by roast turkey, then sweetbreads, removed by beef collops *à la Tortue* served with various vegetables. That was the first course. The second consisted of roast partridge, removed by guinea fowl and snipe, followed by mince pies, cheesecakes, apricot tart, a caramel basket of meringues and a Chantilly cake.

Then the cloth was taken off and Patricia sighed with relief as the fruit and nuts were placed on the polished table, along with the silver trolley containing decanters of port, Lisbon, and Madeira.

She said she would leave him to his

port, and escaped thankfully upstairs to the nursery.

'My dear Miss Patricia,' exclaimed Miss Simpkin, 'my lord will expect you in the drawing room!'

'Nonsense, Simpers. *You* know and *I* know that all that business of the gentlemen joining the ladies after dinner is a polite fiction. They never finish until they fall under the table. Even the Reverend Jessamy had to be scooped off the floor the last time he was here. I do think Firkin is wonderful, all those polite lies he tells so well.' Firkin was the butler. Patricia lowered her voice.

' *"The Reverend Mr Jessamy has been taken poorly by a fit of the colic, Mrs Jessamy, and awaits you in the carriage. The Honourable Mr Brian Pettifor begs leave to tell you, Miss Pettifor, that he has had one of his dizzy spells and awaits you in the carriage."* And all the ladies murmur, *"Of course, poor John, and James, or Brian,"* and I stand at the door and kiss them good-bye and hope *so* sincerely that poor John or James or Brian's malady will soon disappear. I shall not see horrible Lord Charles again this evening. Do you know, he is going to engage a dragon to teach me

21

geometry and dreadful useless things like that. I fear he is going to replace you!'

'*Oh...oh...oh!*' screamed Miss Simpkin, going into strong hysterics.

'What is the meaning of this?' demanded a cross voice from the doorway. Lord Charles stood there, his broad shoulders filling the frame, looking at the scene—Patricia blushing, Miss Simpkin hysterical, and old Nanny Evans snoring through the whole thing.

'I told Miss Simpkin you were going to get some other governess,' said Patricia defiantly.

'I did not say I would turn her out,' he snapped. 'Control yourself, Miss Simpkin. Patricia, you had no right to come up here. I expected you in the drawing room, and out of courtesy followed you there after a few moments. I should have known that courtesy would be wasted on someone as heedless and thoughtless as you. Go downstairs immediately and leave me to reassure Miss Simpkin.'

'You shall not bully her!' cried Patricia, clenching her fists.

'I shall not upset her.' He stood aside and held open the door. 'Downstairs, immediately, Patricia!'

Miss Simpkin was now sobbing quietly. Patricia threw her a helpless look and left the room. As soon as she was in the drawing room, she ran to the mirror and studied her reflection. How strange! She was looking every bit as beautiful as ever. Why was Lord Charles being so nasty to her?

She plumped down on a sofa, put her chin on her hand, and thought furiously. The only thing she could possibly think of doing was to make life so miserable for Lord Charles that he would leave. When this governess-creature arrived, well, she would soon be routed.

She was so engrossed in plots and schemes that she did not even notice Lord Charles entering the room. He was tired and worried. He studied Patricia as she sat deep in thought by the fire. With her hair properly dressed and in a gown more suited to her tender years, he felt sure she would look quite beautiful. The combination of gold hair shot with faint red lights and large dark brown eyes and a creamy skin could be devastating.

He did not blame her for being vain and empty-headed. Those two old doting retainers upstairs were enough to addle any child's wits. And she *was* a child, a child who had learned to please the gentlemen with her pretty parlour tricks.

'Do you play the pianoforte, Miss Patricia?' he asked.

She started at the sound of his deep voice and stood up. 'Of course,' she said.

'Then I should like to hear you play.'

'First tell me about poor Miss Simpkin.'

'Miss Simpkin has nothing to worry about. She has been with you since you were little more than a baby, and I do not believe in turning off servants when their usefulness is over. She will continue to instruct you in lighter subjects such as needlework and watercolour painting while she enjoys a well-earned semi-retirement.

'As you know, under the terms of your father's will your fortune remains in my hands until you are either twenty-one or married. Needless to say, should you marry before you are twenty-one, then it must be to a man of whom I approve.

'I shall stay here only until I think you have improved enough to make your come-out on your seventeenth birthday. I have my own estates to manage.'

'Your wife will miss you,' said Patricia hopefully.

'I am not married.'

'Well, I suppose that does not surprise me.'

'Curb that tongue of yours, miss. Now, play something before I lose my temper.'

His manner was very much that of a tired adult speaking to a spoiled child.

Patricia sat down at the piano and began to murder the music by banging angrily on the keys. But she loved music too much to continue making a mess of it, and settled down to play a piece of Scarlatti as well as any professional musician. Then her fingers moved softly across the keys as she accompanied herself in a sentimental ballad. Her soprano voice, as clear as a bell and as sexless as a choirboy's, sang of lost love and near-forgotten summers.

There was a long silence when she had finished.

'You are a highly talented girl,' Lord Charles said at last. 'I am sure that with the correct schooling you may do very well. You may now go to bed.'

Patricia, although furious at being ordered to bed, was glad to escape.

She stood in the hall boiling with fury. He should be punished. He had looked tired. Then make him even more tired!

She went into the library, which had been used as a living room when her father was alive. It now smelled faintly of disuse, as Patricia used the drawing room and dining room for entertaining guests and preferred to spend her own leisure hours in the nursery. No doubt Lord Charles would think it shocking that a sixteen year-old should play hostess.

She went to a glass case displaying a selection of stuffed animals in the corner of the room. The back of the case had a wooden panel on hinges. She let it down, reached inside, and took out a fine specimen of a stuffed hedgehog.

Then she went back into the hall. The butler, Firkin, was crossing to the drawing room with a decanter of wine on a tray.

Patricia quickly hid the hedgehog behind her back.

'Where have you put Lord Charles?' she asked.

'In the Blue Room in the east wing, miss.'

'I trust Lord Charles will not bully the servants, Firkin?'

'Oh, no, miss.' Firkin looked shocked. 'Very fond of Lord Charles was poor Mr Patterson, your father. Called him a gentleman of good sense.'

'Then why is it that I have never met this gentleman of such good sense before?'

'He came on a visit when you were about seven years old, miss. Stands to reason you wouldn't remember him. You were in the nursery for most of his visit.'

'We were very comfortable before *he* came,' said Patricia.

'Now, miss, do not be in such a taking. You'll find out that his lordship knows what's best for everybody.'

The butler went on his way and Patricia darted up the stairs to the east wing. She opened the door of the Blue Room and went inside. Two tall candles were burning on the toilet table. His lordship's nightshirt was draped over a chair in front of the fire to warm it.

She crossed to a bureau opposite the bed. There was a miniature on top of the bureau of a beautiful, dark-haired woman. 'So *that's* why he is not married,' said Patricia, nodding her head wisely. 'Unrequited love.' She had read of such cases in the novels she loved to devour. His jewel box stood open and she stared in amazement at the glorious assortment of rings and stick pins and diamond buttons.

'At least he must be very rich,' thought Patricia, 'unless he has already started spending *my* money on himself.'

Then she crossed to the bed and flung back the blankets and sheets. She carefully placed the stuffed hedgehog where she estimated his feet would be when he lay down, covered up the bed again, and retreated to the nursery to have a long and delicious gossip with Miss Simpkin, who declared herself to be dizzy with relief that she was not to leave her beloved Miss Patricia after all. Nanny had woken up and demanded to hear all about Lord Charles.

Meanwhile, Lord Charles had decided to go to bed. He would travel to London in the morning and ask his married friends if they knew of a suitable governess.

Firkin and one of the first footmen lighted his way to bed.

The butler made a clucking sound of disapproval. He walked forward and straightened the bedclothes and then turned down the blankets and sheet at one corner in the way they were supposed to be. He privately resolved to give the chambermaid, Mary, a stern lecture as soon as he got back downstairs.

Lord Charles watched him thoughtfully. He picked up one of the candles from the toilet table and looked at the bed.

'I am sorry everything was not just so, my lord,' said Firkin. 'I cannot understand it. My girls are very well trained.'

'Never mind, Firkin,' said Lord Charles. 'That will be all. Oh, by the way where does Miss Patricia sleep?'

'Miss Patricia has the Rose Room in the west wing, my lord.'

'And *is* it rose? This is called the Blue Room and yet there isn't any blue in it. The walls are Nile green.'

'Ah, that is because everything was repainted the year before the master and mistress died. But you will find the names of each room on a card in the cardholder on each door. When guests are staying, we put their names on the cards as well, so that it is easy for everyone to know where everyone else is lodged.'

'Very sensible. Thank you, Firkin. I shall be leaving for London in the morning and I hope to return in a week's time.'

'Very good, my lord. I shall send your man-servant up to you.'

'No, leave him. We had a long journey and I am quite capable of looking after myself. Do not touch my boots. I prefer to clean them. But you may take my coat away for brushing.'

The butler hesitated. 'Does Miss Patricia know you are leaving so soon, my lord?'

'No, I only decided to go a short time ago. Do not trouble her with the news until after I have left. Tell the steward, Jackson, to have the estate books ready for me to look at when I come back. Now, that is definitely all.'

Firkin and the footman bowed their way out. Lord Charles again looked thoughtfully at the bed. Then he went over and ripped the bedclothes back. He picked up the stuffed hedgehog and ran a finger slowly over its prickles.

He walked out of the room and along the landing. Patricia's clear laugh, sounded from the nursery above.

He continued on his way to the west wing.

Fifteen minutes later, Patricia bid a fond good night to Nanny Evans and Miss Simpkin. She had not told them of putting the hedgehog in Lord Charles's bed. She knew that even those two indulgent ladies would be shocked. She undressed, grinning to herself as she thought of Lord Charles thrusting his bare feet down on the hedgehog.

She brushed her hair, looking ruefully at the shorn mess. It had been quite long only a week ago, but Patricia had seen one of the new styles in *La Belle Assemblée* and had been convinced she could achieve the same result by cutting her hair herself.

She climbed into bed, blew out the candles, and snuggled down under the blankets.

And then she let out a piercing scream. With a shaking hand she lit the bed candle and groped beneath the bedclothes.

She pulled out the hedgehog and her fear changed to fury.

'Nothing!' she called to the anxious servants outside her door, who were demanding to know why she had screamed. 'I had a nightmare, that is all.'

It was quite a while before her heart stopped thumping against her ribs. She had had a bad fright.

That she might have given Lord Charles an equally bad fright did not occur to her.

'You have not won,' vowed Miss Patricia Patterson. 'I shall get even with you yet, Lord Charles Gaunt!'

TWO

The fact that Lord Charles had gone to London to find her a governess did not cross Patricia's mind when she found out the next morning that he had already left. Although Firkin told her that Lord Charles would return after a week to inspect the estate ledgers, she quickly convinced herself that he had already tired of her and the whole situation, and would only come back for brief visits. After all, yesterday had been his first visit in nine years.

The weather had turned cold and steel-grey, and the farmers spoke of smelling snow on the wind.

Lord Charles's remarks about her appearance still rankled in Patricia's bosom. She was a good needlewoman. She studied all the fashion plates in a great pile of magazines she had amassed and decided to make herself a stately gown in scarlet merino, and to engage the services of a hairdresser.

This involved a five-mile journey to the

nearest town, Barminster, which claimed to boast the finest shops outside London, and where, it was said, a French emigré had set up a hairdressing business. Miss Simpkin enjoyed the outing as much as Patricia. A bolt of red merino was bought and the hairdresser found and requested to present himself on the morrow at Burnham House. Then Patricia and Miss Simpkin went to a pastry cook's to drink tea and eat cakes.

'That is a fine figure of a man,' said Patricia, waving her teaspoon in the direction of a young army captain who was strutting past. The young man looked across at the window at that moment and saw Patricia sitting in the bay. She threw him a roguish look and then demurely lowered her eyes.

'You *are* naughty,' giggled Miss Simpkin. 'Only look! He seems quite *épris.*'

But Patricia abruptly lost interest in the captain.

'Would you say Lord Charles is very old?' she asked.

'No, my dear. A very fine figure of a man. About thirty, I should think.'

'Firkin says he visited us when I was very young.'

'I cannot remember. Such a lot of titled

young men came to stay. Your father dearly loved entertaining, as you know.'

'Is Lord Charles rich?'

'I believe him to be very rich, yes.'

'But I remember you were saying only the other week that he was a younger son. Younger sons don't have money.'

'Let me see,' said Miss Simpkin. 'Oh, do but look! That delicious army captain is still outside, looking at you.'

'No, I don't want to look. Go on.'

'About Lord Charles? Yes, well, his elder brother is the heir when their father, the Earl of Dunster, dies. The countess is dead. Lord Charles fought in the wars against that monster Bonaparte, but he got the fever and had to be sent home. He turned his mind to investments and funds and Consoles, and business things like that—only gentlemen understand that sort of thing. It was said he prospered and became very rich in his own right. He has estates in the North.'

'You are so well informed, Simpers. How do you do it?'

'It is all those county balls and things, my love. Us old chaperones have nothing else to do but gossip while you young things dance. Will you be going to the

34

assembly here next week? Lord Charles was quite shocked that you have been to so many balls when you are not even "out." '

'Even children go to this assembly,' said Patricia. 'Even he cannot object. Simpers, stop looking at that captain. Lord Charles would be quite outraged if he could see you.'

Miss Simpkin giggled and drank her tea. Watching her Patricia began to worry for the first time about whether Miss Simpkin was not too loose and silly in her ways to be in charge of a young girl. She had never really thought of it before. Her mother had not found fault with the governess, but then her mother had hardly ever visited the nursery or the schoolroom. Miss Simpkin was only expected to have Patricia dressed and brushed and presented in the drawing room for half an hour before dinner, before taking her back to the nursery.

Patricia frowned. Her parents had always seemed very fond and loving when she saw them at these specially arranged times. But they had never, even when she was ill, gone out of their way to seek her out and ask after her well-being.

The servants were instructed to wait on

her hand and foot, Miss Simpkin was instructed to see that she had all the novels and magazines, dresses and ribbons her heart desired.

Patricia frowned even more, searching for the memory of perhaps one caress.

'Mama must have held me in her arms and rocked me when I was a baby,' she said suddenly.

Miss Simpkin looked startled. 'Mrs Patterson would not need to do anything like that. You had a wet-nurse, and then of course there was always nanny.'

'I have been brought up by two eccentric aged spinsters,' thought Patricia, and then immediately felt disloyal. Nanny Evans and Miss Simpkin were both diamonds of the first water, and yet...

'Where *did* you come from, Simpers? I never thought to ask. I mean, before you came to Burnham House?'

Miss Simpkin neatly turned the dregs of her tea into her saucer and, tried to read the leaves left in her cup. Then she sighed.

'I was very grateful to get the post. I had had my own seminary in Bath, you know. But...but something happened that gave me an uneasy conscience and...and...I was glad to leave. Please do not ask me any more about it. It was not the happiest of times.'

'Miss Patterson and Miss Simpkin!' The Misses Grant, two dashing local beauties, had just come into the pastry cook's. Emily and Agnes Grant were twins and a few years older than Patricia. Patricia was rather jealous of them, but did not realize it. The girls joined Patricia and her governess and started to ply them with questions about Lord Charles. Patricia was not surprised that they had heard of his visit. Servants' gossip travelled like lightning in the country.

Patricia said he was a bullying ogre, and the sisters laughed and said a rich, unmarried lord must be all that was delightful. Gossip then turned to the fascinating subject of gowns and bonnets.

As Patricia finally rose to leave, she suddenly asked Emily and Agnes, 'Did your mother hug and kiss you much when you were small?'

Both sisters looked startled. 'Of course not,' said Agnes. 'Ladies *never* do that, dear Miss Patterson. Only very common people do *that*. A lady sends for her children from time to time the way she sends for her servants. All the care is left to wet-nurses and nannies. What a very odd question!'

Patricia felt reassured. Her own upbringing appeared to have been perfectly normal. Miss Simpkin was just an ordinary governess. The sisters, for example, seemed to find nothing amiss with her.

But as soon as she left the pastry cook's, Patricia thought, 'When I have children, I will sing lullabies to them and hold them when they are frightened.' The dashing captain swept off his hat as she passed, but Patricia did not even notice him. 'Perhaps I am vulgar after all,' she thought. 'It appears that only very common people have a fondness for their children.'

The following day was pleasantly taken up with the hairdresser's visit. He had to stay the whole day because Patricia's hair was put into hot roulers—clay sausage shapes—and he had to wait to take them out and complete the coiffure.

He left the roulers with Patricia, advising her to grow her hair and wear it in looser curls. Since her hair had a natural wave, he said, he thought that once it had grown a certain length, he could cut it in such a way that it would curl naturally.

Patricia was delighted with the effect of the soft hairstyle and only wished the horrible Lord Charles could see how mondaine she looked.

Unfortunately for Patricia, Lord Charles had found a governess very quickly. Married friends, the Lucases, had employed a certain Miss Deborah Sinclair to teach their two boys when the children were very small. The boys were now six and seven respectively and Mr and Mrs Lucas wished to replace her with a male tutor. They praised Miss Sinclair highly. Lord Charles was impressed with the governess's appearance. She was only about a year younger than himself, and had a calm, well-bred air.

She further pleased him by saying she was prepared to leave and take up her duties immediately.

He explained the situation as they drove back to Burnham House. Patricia, he said, had been sadly spoiled. She must have lessons and more lessons. She must stop her hoydenish ways so that he could put her on the Marriage Market as soon as was decently possible. Girls like Patricia quieted down when they were respectably married.

Miss Sinclair sat listening quietly, admiring his lordship's deep voice and handsome profile.

'You will also find,' said Lord Charles, 'that her doting nanny and present governess will try to continue to spoil her. Try not to offend them. Report any interference to me and let me deal with it. Patricia must be disciplined. If she is allowed to go on the way she *has* been going on, she will probably run off with the first half-pay rattle in a scarlet coat who takes her fancy.

'Furthermore, her clothes are not suitable for her age and her hair is a mess. She will need schooling in order to present a modest appearance.

'At first sight, she may appear silly and vain, and yet she plays the pianoforte like an angel. No one can play like that unless they have a great deal of sensitivity and intelligence.'

'I shall do my best,' said Miss Sinclair. 'Miss Patterson will be expecting me?'

'No, I left without telling her I was going or why I was going. I left word with the butler that I would be gone for a week, but I have been away only four days. As I told you, Burnham House is only a day's drive. We shall be there a little after nightfall. You will take your meals in the family dining room, Miss Sinclair. Patricia needs to be schooled as much at table as in the schoolroom.'

Miss Sinclair turned pink with pleasure. The salary he had offered her was very generous and now she was to be treated like a lady instead of like an upper servant. Miss Sinclair sent up a silent prayer to God to aid her in the breaking of Patricia Patterson's rebellious spirit, to aid her in pleasing this wonderful aristocrat who was treating her with such courtesy and kindness.

Miss Sinclair was not, however, prepared to discover that Miss Patricia Patterson was a raving beauty.

Nor, for that matter, was Lord Charles.

The scarlet merino gown, with its simple classic lines and modest neckline was a miracle of dressmaking. Instead of clashing with the colour of her hair, it appeared to enhance it. The softer hairstyle of loose curls prettily framed her face, making her look like a Botticelli angel.

There was also a subtle air of hauteur about her which disconcerted Miss Sinclair. It did not disconcert Lord Charles, who was shrewder than Miss Sinclair and knew that the new *grande dame* manner was adopted.

Things went smoothly at dinner. Lord Charles and Miss Sinclair discoursed on the political topics of the day, while Patricia maintained her stately manner but privately thought she would die of boredom.

Trouble did not start until the following morning when Miss Sinclair roused Patricia from a deep sleep and told her to present herself in the schoolroom. Patricia yawned and went back to sleep.

Miss Sinclair shook Patricia awake again, and Patricia threw a pillow at the governess's head.

Miss Sinclair returned with two chambermaids. Patricia haughtily told them to leave her bedchamber immediately. But Lord Charles had informed the staff in no uncertain terms that Miss Sinclair was to have absolute control of Patricia and that the governess's word was law. At a nod from Miss Sinclair, the chambermaids tipped the amazed and shocked Patricia out of bed, and then showed every sign of dressing her by force.

Pushing them out of the room in a fury and slamming the door, Patricia scrambled into her clothes after a token wash and presented herself in the schoolroom.

Miss Sinclair looked thoughtfully at the clay roulers in Patricia's hair and told her to go and remove them. Miss Patterson must present herself in the schoolroom looking neat and fully dressed, *not* in her undress.

Patricia ranted and screamed that she was mistress in her own house and would do as she pleased. Miss Sinclair simply went out of the schoolroom and locked Patricia in, saying she might stay there until she had come to her senses.

Patricia just could not believe all this was happening. Miss Simpkin came to the door and stood outside, crying helplessly, but hiccupping there was nothing she could do. The hours passed into the afternoon. Patricia was hungry and bored.

At last, she forced open the window, which had jammed with the damp, and climbed down the ivy.

Snow was beginning to fall, delicate, glittering, feathery flakes. Patricia shivered and walked along the terrace to let herself in through the french windows of the drawing room.

But there they were, Miss Sinclair and

Lord Charles, sitting on either side of a blazing fire, making as pretty and cozy a picture as anyone—other than Miss Patricia Patterson—could wish to see. Lord Charles was reading a newspaper and Miss Sinclair was knitting, her long white fingers holding the steel pins. Her heavy brown hair was wound into a neat coil at the nape of the neck. Her gown was dove grey. She looked the epitome of domestic femininity.

Lord Charles lowered his paper and said something and Miss Sinclair smiled. Lord Charles put down his newspaper, stood up, and threw another log on the fire. Firkin entered with the tea tray and set the silver pot and the pretty blue and gold cups down in front of Miss Sinclair. She smiled on him graciously.

The rising wind tugged at Patricia's gown, but so incandescent with rage was she that she did not feel the cold. From the terrace she picked up a plant in its heavy stone pot and hurled it through the window.

There was a tremendous shattering of glass. Splinters flew all over the room.

Lord Charles leaped through the giant gaping hole in the french window, seized

Patricia, and shook her till her teeth rattled.

He dragged her screaming, yelling, and kicking into the drawing room and then into the hall. He sat down in a carved oak chair, slung her over his knee, took off his thin leather show, and applied it forcefully to Patricia's bottom.

All the fight went out of Patricia and she began to cry dismally. Lord Charles set her on her feet.

'Now, will you behave?' he roared.

The drawing room door was open. The curtains billowed out about the jagged hole in the window. Firkin and Miss Sinclair stood as if turned to stone. The enormity of what she had done made Patricia begin to tremble.

For almost the first time in her life, she apologized. 'I am sorry,' she whispered. 'But I am not used to such harsh treatment.'

She stood, shaken, the tears running down her face.

All at once, Lord Charles's anger left him. He felt sorry for her. It was not her fault she had been so spoiled.

'You may lead a very comfortable and easy life if you will only do as you are told. Miss Sinclair will take you to the schoolroom and there you will begin your lessons. Tea will be sent up to you.'

Lord Charles heard the sound of carriage wheels. 'Callers,' he said. 'Firkin, put them in the library. Miss Sinclair, take Patricia up to the schoolroom.'

In ten minutes' time, the Misses Grant and their mother were warmly esconced by the library fire, eyes shining with excitement as they surveyed this rich and handsome addition to the neighbourhood.

'I am sorry Miss Patricia cannot be with us,' said Lord Charles.

The sisters looked at him hopefully, but they saw he had no intention of explaining where Patricia was or what she was doing.

'We are come,' said Agnes, 'to see if Patricia still intends to go to the ball at Barminster.'

'When is this ball to be held?'

'In two days' time.'

'I think,' said Lord Charles, 'that my ward is a trifle young to attend balls. She has not yet made her come-out.'

'It is different in the country,' said Mrs Grant placidly. 'It is only the local assembly at Barminster. Everyone goes, even the very young children.'

'Then perhaps I shall escort her myself,' smiled Lord Charles.

Patricia was immediately forgotten in all the excitement this statement produced. Both Emily and Agnes was anxious to cut a dash by securing at least one dance with this most eligible lord. Conversation rattled on happily over the teacups until Mrs Grant indicated to her reluctant daughters that it was time to leave.

Lord Charles sat for a long time in the library after they had left. The Grant girls were pretty and frivolous and very like Patricia on the surface. He began to feel ashamed of himself. He had never struck a female in the whole of his life, and the more he thought about it, the more he became convinced he had behaved like a monster. Patricia *had* behaved disgracefully. But there were other ways of disciplining her.

He finally took himself up to the schoolroom where Patricia sat bending a tear-stained face over her lessons.

'I hear there is to be a ball in Barminster,' he said. 'I have decided you may attend, Patricia. In fact, I shall escort you myself.'

She looked at him coldly and said, 'And

to think I was looking forward to it.' Then she bent her head over her books again.

Lord Charles slammed his way out of the schoolroom, all new, kind thoughts about Patricia utterly gone.

Snow fell that day and the next. Lord Charles found himself hoping that roads would be blocked so that he would not have to take that pert minx to the ball.

But on the Friday, the day of the ball, a thaw set in and a watery sun struggled through the clouds. By afternoon, the skies were calm and blue. The roads were clear and there was to be a full moon that night.

When she was not in the schoolroom, Patricia had spent the rest of the time shut up in her bedroom. Lord Charles assumed she was preparing some grand toilette for the ball.

But Patricia was planning revenge.

She did not hate Miss Sinclair, considering her a colourless creature who was merely obeying Lord Charles's every order. Anyone with more spirit would have felt some compassion for a beautiful pupil condemned to spend long hours in the classroom, thought Patricia, who could not bear to admit to herself that she was actually beginning to enjoy those terrible lessons.

But Patricia *did* hate Lord Charles. Now that the shock of breaking the window was over, all her remorse had fled. Lord Charles had struck her, and for that he must be punished.

At first, Patricia toyed with the idea of killing him, but could not really think of a safe method of doing away with him. Growing weary at last with useless plots, she decided to escape into the works of one of her favourite authors, Miss Louisa Sydney Stanhope. The new volumes of her latest work, *The Confessional of Valombre,* had arrived just that day from the Minerva Press.

Patricia opened the page and plunged in. The first paragraph surely described such a man as Lord Charles Gaunt.

'It was at the close of the festival of St Fabian, when the last sonorous tone of the organ had ceased, and the pale glimmer of the tape had expired, when nature had sealed the eyes of fanaticism, and even the vigil virgin had ceased to watch, that a stranger paused at the gate of the convent of Valombre...'

The dressing bell sounded and Patricia

dropped the book and glanced at the clock in amazement. Time had passed quickly while she had searched her mind for ways of revenge. As she dressed, she now saw Lord Charles as the villain of a Gothic novel. He looked satanic. He had black hair and green eyes. He was pitiless. He had struck her. He was a monster.

This villain, this fantasy of a cruel monster, was very comforting and much more reassuring than any real-life guardian who had struck her in a temper because she had smashed the drawing room window.

She had altered a ballgown for the occasion, removing most of the bows and frills which she had realized made it overfussy. Her ensemble consisted of a simple underdress of straw silk with a white gauze overdress embroidered with gold. A gold tiara studded with large topazes was set among her curls and a topaz and gold necklace was clasped around her neck.

When she finally joined Lord Charles in the drawing room, it was to find him cross at her tardiness, and he looked more like the villain of her fantasies than ever. She shivered with Gothic fear and Lord Charles asked her testily if she were cold.

He was wearing a black evening coat

and black silk breeches. His long white waistcoat was embroidered with silver, and diamonds sparkled on his fingers, in his stock, and on the buttons of his coat.

Lord Charles was tempted to tell Patricia to go upstairs again and put on jewellery more suited to a girl of her years, but she looked so scared and downcast that he had not the heart to criticize her.

Their arrival at the assembly caused a small sensation. As she removed her mantle in the cloakroom, Patricia was besieged with questions about Lord Charles. All the ladies declared him to be divinely handsome, which the cynical Patricia translated in her mind as 'divinely rich.'

She was surprised that some of the girls of her age kept insisting that Lord Charles was the most good-looking man they had ever seen. He was so very *old*, thought Patricia, quite in his dotage, and steeped in dark sin, she reminded herself.

Patricia was soon surrounded by a court of admirers when she entered the ballroom. Among them was the handsome captain who had looked at her through the window of the pastry cook's.

He was only about twenty, and had thick, curling brown hair and a roguish eye. She danced with him twice and then let him lead her into supper.

The captain's name was Peter Oxford. He flattered her with compliments and said he hoped to ask her guardian for permission to call on her.

'He will never give permission to you or any other gentleman,' said Patricia sadly.

'I am of a good family!'

'That is not what I meant.' Patricia avoided Lord Charles's reproving glare, glad he was on the other side of the room, and drank a huge gulp of wine.

'Then what is the matter? Does he want you for himself?'

Patricia remembered a delicious novel she had read the year before, when a wicked guardian had tried, in order to gain her fortune, to force his ward to marry him. She drank some more wine.

'Alas,' she said, lowering her voice to a dramatic whisper, 'I am afraid he does. He tyrannizes me, and only this week he...he *beat* me!'

'An angel like yourself? I shall call him out!'

'He would never meet you,' said Patricia sadly. 'He would report you to your commanding officer.'

'Coward!'

'He is insufferably arrogant. Only see how he stares at me, his eyes full of venom.'

The captain looked across the room and met the cold, green glare of Lord Charles Gaunt.

'Gad's, Oonds! He looks like the devil. My poor Miss Patterson.'

Patricia drank more wine. 'I cannot escape,' she said. 'There is no one to help me. He has engaged a sort of woman jailor. Most of the time I am kept locked in the schoolroom.'

'Monstrous! You are not a child.'

'I am nineteen,' said Patricia, quickly adding three years to her age. Her head swam pleasantly with the wine she had drunk. She was enjoying her story. It was quite like living in a book.

The captain had drunk a great deal himself. He was bewitched by Patricia, by her huge pansy eyes, by the creaminess of her skin, and by the odd colour of her hair.

'I would snatch you away from him!' cried the captain.

'But if I marry without his consent, I do

not get a penny of my fortune until I am twenty-one,'

'Two years to go,' thought the captain. 'A fortune and all this beauty!'

Aloud, he said, 'I have my pay and an allowance from my father. We could marry. The married people in my regiment always have comfortable quarters.'

Patricia sobered slightly. All at once she saw how to revenge herself on Lord Charles. If she ran away with this young man, Lord Charles would be shamed and humiliated. Furthermore, it would be wonderful to be married to a handsome young captain who would pet her and fuss over her. Patricia saw the captain as a sort of masculine combination of Miss Simpkin and Nanny Evans. It would be fun playing house. She would entertain his friends. She would be the toast of the regiment. The Prince Regent would get to hear of her beauty...

'We could run away,' she said lightly.

The captain prided himself on being a man of action. 'Why don't we run away *now*,' he said. 'We could rack up at some inn. I'll go back to my barracks for a day or two until the fuss dies down and we can be married by special license.'

'*Now?*' said Patricia, her eyes very wide.

'Why not?' he grinned. 'Now or never, I should think, from the furious look on your guardian's face.'

Patricia felt elated and breathless. Good-bye to lessons. Good-bye to humiliation and being treated as a slave.

'Yes,' she said. 'I *will* marry you. But how do we leave the ballroom without his following us?'

'Spill some wine down your gown and dab at it and make a fuss. Then excuse yourself as if you are going to go and clean it. Get your cloak and meet me outside. I'll leave the minute Lord Charles takes his eye off me, which he surely will once you have left.'

Patricia jerked her wine glass and spilled it on the gauze of her gown. She jumped up with a little shriek and started dabbing at herself with a napkin.

'Now look what she's done,' said Lord Charles crossly to his supper companion, Miss Emily Grant.

'Soda water is the best thing to remove a wine stain,' said Emily. 'Oh, she is leaving to go to the cloakroom. I shall go and help her.'

'You are very kind, Miss Grant,' said

Lord Charles. 'Give her a message from me, pray. She is to drink no more this evening.'

Eager to please, Emily hurried off.

Patricia was not pleased to see her. In fact, she looked furious.

'What do *you* want?' she asked nastily. 'Has Lord Charles sent you to spy on me?'

'I only came to help you,' said Emily. 'He wants you to stop drinking wine. He told me to tell you so,' she added with a toss of her head.

'Why do you not mind your own business,' said Patricia, desperate to have her gone. She realized she had never liked the Grant girls. They were relative newcomers to the county and the gentlemen were apt to be very silly and spoony about Emily and Agnes, calling them beautiful and nonsense like that. The fact that Patricia's nose had been decidedly put out of joint by their arrival did not occur to her.

She flicked a curl in the mirror and said maliciously over her shoulder, 'Go back to Lord Charles. You should suit very well. He is old and you, dear Emily, are dull.'

'Oooh! I *hate* you!' Emily stormed out of the cloakroom.

No sooner had she gone than Patricia snatched up her mantle and slipped out to the front of the inn where the captain was waiting.

'Let us go, Miss Patterson,' he said gaily. 'Our life together has just begun!'

THREE

Deborah Sinclair gave a little sigh. She studied her reflection thoughtfully in the glass. She was, she decided, quite a fine-looking woman. Her nose, which others of lesser perception and gentility might condemn as being a trifle too long, was, in fact, she decided, an outward manifestation of her inward good breeding. Her slightly prominent eyes were large and blue, not a vulgar bright blue, but an interestingly pale colour.

Her waist was trim and her bosom generous. She raised her skirt an inch. Her ankles were slim and neat enough to please the highest stickler.

She had hoped Lord Charles might have asked her to attend the ball as chaperone. But he had seemed to think his own presence enough.

She had been surprised to find that Patricia was an apt pupil. The girl had an amazingly retentive memory.

She could not help hoping that Patricia

would behave badly at the ball. It would be pleasant if Lord Charles sent for her on his return and asked her advice.

She decided to ring for tea and cakes and pass the long evening reading some improving work.

She pulled the bellrope.

Down in the kitchen, Firkin looked up from cleaning the silver and glared at the row of metal bells on the wall.

'Governess's room,' said James, the first footman.

'Let her ring,' said Firkin sourly.

Mrs Miles, the housekeeper, threw him an anxious look. 'Better see what she wants,' said Mrs Miles, 'or she'll go whining to his lordship.'

'I'll 'pologize from the bottom of my heart and say the bell wire must have been broke,' said Firkin. 'Lord Charles is master here now, and it is pleasant to have a man in charge stead o' Miss Patricia and her flighty ways, but that's not to say I agree with his lordship for giving that long-nosed governess leave to order us about.

'I can't help feeling sorry for Miss Patricia. All that book learning. It don't make sense. Education is wasted on girls. Poor Miss Simpkin's near broke her heart.'

'But you always said Miss Patricia could do with a touch of the birch rod,' said Mrs Miles. The bell jangled again. ''Specially when she put that essence o' senna pods in your port and said she was funning.'

'Me complaining is one thing,' said the butler darkly. 'I been here twenty year and Miss Patricia owns the place. It goes against the grain to see her being ordered about by a stranger.' The bell jangled loud and long. 'When them chambermaids told me they was told by Miss Sinclair to tip Miss Patricia out o' bed, I went to Lord Charles and complained. 'Good God, man,' he says. 'I ain't having her locked up in a cupboard all day or beaten with a broom handle like what *I* got in the nursery.' And there's the answer, if you ask me, Mrs Miles. He had that rotten a time 'isself when he was young, stands to reason he thinks she's being treated well.'

The bell jangled furiously.

'Let it ring,' said Firkin. 'That one's got hopes of being my lady and it's all his lordship's fault for elevating her above her station. Lord Charles is a fine man and as sweet a master as any servant could wish, but it's up to us to put that governess in her place. I do wish she would stop ringing. It makes my head ache something terrible.'

'*I* should have accompanied Miss Patricia to the ball,' sniffed Miss Simpkin as she sat in front of the nursery fire with Nanny Evans. 'I always go. Well, I suppose I should be thankful he didn't invite *her*. Poor baby, poor Patricia. All those dry, dry lessons. Patricia should rest after the ball tomorrow, but that horrible Sinclair woman told me she intends to have her out of bed and into the schoolroom at seven as usual. Oh, if only I could stop her.'

Nanny Evans lumbered up from her rocking chair and took a green glass bottle down from the mantelpiece.

'Take her a cup of tea and put some of this in it,' she cackled.

'What is it?' asked Miss Simpkin.

'Laudanum.'

'*Oh, no, I couldn't!*'

'Suit yourself,' said Nanny Evans, sitting down again and beginning to close her eyes.

The door of the nursery opened and Miss Sinclair appeared. She was flushed and upset.

'I do not know what is up with the servants,' she said. 'I rang and rang for tea and no one answered.'

Nanny Evans opened her eyes. 'Then go down to the kitchens and see what's up.'

'It is not my place to do so,' said Miss Sinclair haughtily. She turned to Miss Simpkin. *'You go.'*

'And why should I go when you will not?' demanded Miss Simpkin, colouring up under her rouge.

'Because I am a *real* governess and you are more of a nursemaid,' said Miss Sinclair.

Nanny Evans gave Miss Simpkin a toothless grin and glanced up at the green bottle on the mantel.

Miss Sinclair regretted her words almost as soon as they were uttered, but Miss Simpkin said mildly, 'There is no need to trouble the servants. We have just made some tea, the best Bohea. Go to your rooms and I shall bring it to you.'

'You must not trouble yourself,' said Miss Sinclair. 'I shall take it with me.'

'No, no,' said Miss Simpkin, pushing her towards the door with surprising force. 'I shall bring it to you.'

When she had gone, Miss Simpkin took down the green glass bottle, poured a large spoonful into a teacup, and then added the tea, which was strong and dark in colour.

Nanny Evans cackled again.

Lord Charles entered the ballroom with Emily on his arm. Emily had merely told him that Patricia had refused her help. She felt it would not be ladylike to criticize Miss Patricia to her guardian.

To her disappointment, Lord Charles bowed and left her before the next dance had even started.

Lord Charles made his way around the room, looking for Patricia. The ballroom was very crowded. There were children playing among the feet of the guests. There were elderly couples sitting in corners, talking to their friends. Young country bucks were ogling pretty girls, and there was a sprinkling of scarlet coats showing that a regiment was billeted nearby.

It took Lord Charles some time to realize there was no sign of either Patricia or the young captain who had taken her in for supper.

The assembly was held in the ballroom of Barminster's best inn. Lord Charles searched all the anterooms and even the cloakrooms set aside for the ladies. No Patricia.

Anxious to avert any scandal and convinced now that she was dallying in the courtyard outside with her military gallant, Lord Charles decided to go outside and look for them himself.

There had been a fresh shower of snow during the evening, but once more the sky was clear and a bright moon shone down on the sparkling courtyard. Unlike at a London ball, guests at a country assembly came at the beginning and left at the very end. The ostlers, grooms, and coachmen were all snug in the tap.

Only two pairs of footprints marred the pristine white of the snow, one set made by a woman with small feet wearing slippers, the other by a man wearing dancing pumps. Lord Charles followed the trail through the silent night streets of Barminster. At times the prints were crossed and recrossed by other steps, but there were so few people abroad it was easy to follow the original prints.

At one stage, the prints disappeared altogether, or so he thought. He stood, puzzled, looking this way and that. A link boy passed with his torch on the other side of the street under the overhanging eaves of the old buildings, and Lord Charles saw the prints again, on the opposite side of the street. The marks on the road itself had been blurred by passing carts and carriages.

He followed them down a mean, narrow sidestreet as far as the door of a sleazy-looking inn. There were loud voices and coarse laughter coming from the tap. He hesitated only for a moment, wishing he had his cloak to cover his jewels and evening finery, before going into the inn.

There was a small dark hall with the door to the tap on one side and the door to the coffee room on the other. Straight ahead was a rickety flight of stairs.

The open door of the coffee room showed it to be deserted. Patricia would hardly be in the tap and in such company. A voice was raised in a bawdy song.

Lord Charles began to mount the stairs.

Everything had seemed like a marvellous adventure to Patricia, until she reached the outside of the inn.

'Does it have to be here?' she asked, drawing back a little. 'It looks very dirty.'

'Only for one night,' said Captain Peter Oxford. 'I'll move you to somewhere better tomorrow, but the big hunt will be on tonight. The landlord here will never give us away. I'll pay him well to keep his mouth shut.'

For one moment, Patricia thought of turning around and running away. But then she remembered that smacking, and set her lips in a firm line and let the captain usher her into the hallway.

'You stay here,' said the captain. 'Be back in a moment.'

Patricia waited anxiously, listening to the loud voices in the tap. Fortunately, she did not have to wait long. The captain came out of the tap brandishing a large key and with two bottles of brandy under his arm.

'All set,' he said cheerfully. 'We've got a room.'

Patricia stumbled up the dark stair after him. He groped around until he found the keyhole, and then led her into a room barred with moonlight from the curtainless window.

He kicked the door shut behind them and after several fumblings and scrapings with his tinderbox managed to light a candle.

The room was very bare. There was a large bed in one corner without curtains or canopy, a deal table, and two chairs. A fire was laid in the grate which the captain lit.

He then pulled two thick tumblers out of his pockets.

'We cannot stay here together,' said Patricia, shivering. 'We are not married *yet.*'

'It's only for one night,' said the captain, tossing his hat on the bed. 'Nobody will know we've been here and the landlord won't talk.'

'But we cannot share a bed.'

He looked at her impatiently. 'You sleep in it, and I'll lie on top of the cover.' He poured himself a large tumbler of brandy, tossed it off, and then poured himself another.

To add to her troubles, Patricia realized she was in a certain amount of physical discomfort.

'I am afraid I must...I have to...oh, I cannot explain.'

'What?'

'I have to...*you* know.'

'There's a chamberpot under the bed.'

'*Sir!*'

'Very well. It's downstairs and out through the back, in the yard.'

'But what if I meet some of those terrible men from the tap?'

'You won't. They go out in the street.' He poured himself another glass of brandy.

Patricia lit another candle and made her way downstairs and into the freezing cold of the yard.

She knew now she could not go through with it. She would tell him so as soon as she got back upstairs, and then make her escape. She did not know what excuse she was going to give Lord Charles for her absence, but she was sure she would be able to think of something before she saw him again.

She hurried up the stairs again, quickening her step as she heard the sound of voices below.

She let herself into the bedroom and then stood appalled. She had not been away very long, but in that short time the captain had taken off all his clothes, fallen naked on the bed over next to the wall, and gone to sleep; or more likely, thought Patricia looking at the remains of the brandy, passed out.

She gave a shocked squeak and averted her eyes from his naked body.

She would just need to leave without speaking to him.

But, as she went down the stairs, three

men emerged from the tap, all very drunk. She shrank back into the shadow of the staircase.

The captain simply must wake up, must help her.

Patricia retreated back into the room. Fresh air. That was the thing. She opened the window and let a blast of icy air into the room.

Then, half-closing her eyes, she crossed to the bed and seized one naked shoulder and shook hard.

'Wake up!' she said. 'Oh, please wake up.'

But Captain Oxford had had a great deal to drink before he even went to the ball and much more at it. He was one of those young men who can drink much and appear sober for some hours before collapsing, suddenly and dramatically, dead drunk.

Patricia seized the water jug and poured the contents over the captain.

He leaped out of bed shouting a string of oaths.

'You must get me out of here!' screamed Patricia.

He looked at her in a dazed way, looked at his naked body, stretched out his arms, and said, 'Darling, you are wonderful.'

'You're drunk!' raged Patricia. 'We never *did* anything. Oh, get your clothes on.'

He stood staring at her stupidly, rocking backward and forward on the balls of his feet.

There came the sound of someone mounting the stairs. Patricia whirled about, ran to the door, and turned the key in the lock.

'Patricia!' came Lord Charles's voice.

'What have I done?' she whispered. 'He'll *kill* us.'

'Who...he?' demanded the captain, blinking like an owl.

'Get your clothes on,' said Patricia desperately, as an angry fist started pounding at the door.

Like a man moving in a dream, he pulled on his shirt and drawers and stockings.

'Oh, *hurry,*' said Patricia, ashen with fright.

'Breeches. Where?' demanded the captain, looking about the room.

'Here!' Patricia picked them up. 'I will help you. Get them on.'

He sat down in a chair and pulled on his breeches and then stood up with them at half mast.

Patricia seized the Inexpressibles and tried to pull them up around his waist.

'My sweet,' murmured the captain drunkenly, kissing the back of her neck.

With a terrible crack the lock splintered and the door flew wide.

The scene that met Lord Charles's eyes was worse than anything he had anticipated. Patricia appeared to be fumbling with the captain's breeches while he kissed the back of her neck.

All in that moment, the captain looked up. He saw the naked fury in Lord Charles's eyes, saw his fist come up, and sobered in an instant.

He turned and made a flying leap through the window.

Patricia ran and looked out. The captain was lying on his back in the snow, staring up in an amazed way at the moon. Then, as Lord Charles dragged Patricia aside and looked out himself, the captain staggered to his feet and lurched off into the darkness.

Lord Charles left the window to run down the stairs, but his way was blocked by the burly landlord who was clutching a cudgel.

'Break my property, would 'ee?' he said. His eyes fastened on Lord Charles's diamonds and a look of pure greed lit up his eyes.

He lumbered forward, raising the cudgel. Lord Charles sprang nimbly to one side as the cudgel came down, whirled about, drove his fist hard into the landlord's face. The landlord sat down with a surprised grunt.

Lord Charles seized Patricia roughly by the arm. 'Come, you slut...*jade*...slut!' He dragged her down the stairs, shouldering his way past a group of men who had gathered at the bottom, and then hauled her out into the night.

'I have left my mantle,' said Patricia, shivering with cold and fright.

'That is not all you have left,' he said grimly. 'Was ever a man so plagued?'

She tried to escape him, but he twisted her arm behind her back and hustled her along in the direction of the assembly.

Once there, he rousted his coachman and grooms out of the tap, still holding firmly on to Patricia. He held her while the coach was brought around, and then he wrenched open the door and threw her inside.

'You are ruined!' he said savagely. 'Do you realize that?'

'Nothing happened,' said Patricia, scared but defiant. 'We are to be married.'

'No, you are not. What is his name? I shall see that young man's commanding officer in the morning.'

Patricia set her lips in a mutinous line. She had not known until the last moments that the captain was drunk. She felt responsible for his mad behaviour. She felt a stubborn loyalty towards the foolish young officer.

'We shall go into this matter further,' grated Lord Charles.

It was a miserable journey home for Patricia. She felt cold and wretched. Her rosy, wine-induced dream of freedom had gone. She felt guilty, she felt dirty and soiled. Since the weight of guilt was almost too much to bear, she alleviated it by hating Lord Charles the more. If he had not humiliated her, it would never have happened.

He had erupted into her happy, sunny, carefree life and torn it apart. She would *never* forgive him.

Lord Charles sat gloomily beside her, wondering what on earth to do. He would go see the commanding officer in the morning. Would the young man keep quiet about the affair, or would he need to be paid to keep his mouth shut? But what if the wretched Patricia was pregnant?

Then he thought of Miss Sinclair and heaved a sigh of relief. He was sure she would know exactly what to do.

Lord Charles did not believe in servants working all hours of the night simply because their master was out enjoying himself. He had told Firkin that none of the servants need wake up.

He led Patricia up to her room and locked her in. He then went in search of Miss Sinclair whose room, he was sure, was off the landing between the floor he was on and the floor above. She had made a passing reference to the fact that her room was neither on the family floor nor upstairs on the servants' floor, but tactfully somewhere in between.

Sure enough, there was a polished wood door on a half landing.

He tapped gently on it. 'Miss Sinclair!' he called.

He tried again and again. Miss Sinclair was obviously a heavy sleeper.

He was too worried and anxious, too much in need of some sensible advice, to think of rousing a female servant to open

Miss Sinclair's door and investigate.

He gently turned the handle and went in. He saw a dim figure on the bed and called again. The figure did not move.

Worried in case the governess might be ill, he lit a candle and held it up.

Miss Sinclair was lying fully clothed on the bed. Her mouth was hanging open and she was snoring.

Alarmed, he shook her shoulder. Her eyes slowly opened and she looked up at him. 'Charles, my love,' she said in a slurred voice, and then fell asleep again.

'Drunk!' muttered Lord Charles, feeling as if his last prop had been knocked out from under him.

He was suddenly very tired. He blew out the candle and went slowly down to his own room.

Women!

A whole household of useless, senseless women! He clutched his hair in despair.

Something had to be done about Patricia.

The next day, the nightmare continued for Patricia. Lord Charles returned with the commanding officer of the regiment and together they questioned her. She bravely admitted to being drunk. She said she did not know the name of the officer, only that he had said he was a captain. The guest list of the assembly had already been checked by Lord Charles, who had found to his despair that a simple invitation had gone out to the commanding officer inviting himself and fifteen of his officers. 'Then let the fifteen be brought before me,' Lord Charles had demanded, sure that he would recognize Patricia's officer when he saw him. But the fifteen had all been the worse for wear, and at least seven of them were tall with brown hair. All denied having danced or dined with Patricia. Looking at their faces, and seeing the occasional sly glances exchanged between them, Lord Charles had come to the conclusion that they were banding together to protect the culprit. Now, from the commanding officer's embarrassed face and half-hearted questions, Lord Charles knew he did not really want to get one of his men into trouble.

So the problem of what to do with Patricia remained.

Miss Sinclair had to find out from Patricia herself what had happened. To her amazement, Lord Charles showed no sign of asking her advice. Feeling slightly groggy and wondering why she had slept so heavily—and with her clothes on, too!—Miss Sinclair could not enjoy Patricia's disgrace since it had not encouraged Lord Charles to seek her, Miss Sinclair, out.

Orders came up to the schoolroom that in future Patricia was to have her meals in the nursery and was not to be allowed downstairs.

Miss Sinclair brightened. Rosy fantasies of intimate meals with Lord Charles floated through her head. She presented herself in her best brown silk in the drawing room half an hour before dinner. No Lord Charles. On hearing the dinner bell, she went through to the dining room. Lord Charles was just about to sit down at table. He looked at her with an expression of surprise, mixed with faint distaste.

'Miss Sinclair,' he said, 'I thought I made it clear that Miss Patricia was to take her meals in the nursery.'

'But, my lord, I did not think you meant me as well,' Miss Sinclair blurted out.

He looked at her thoughtfully and she turned scarlet.

Then he picked up his knife and fork and began to eat.

Stammering apologies, Miss Sinclair

backed out of the room. She shared a silent meal in the nursery.

Miss Simpkin felt her beloved Patricia's disgrace keenly. She had tried to romanticize the whole thing, but Patricia had snapped at her that she did not want to think about that disgraceful evening.

Miss Sinclair was just about to retire to bed when Firkin came up to say my lord wished to see her in the drawing room. Hope sprang in her bosom again. She ran so quickly downstairs, she was pink and breathless when she at last stood before Lord Charles.

'Before I begin to discuss the problem of Patricia,' he said, 'I think we had better discuss *your* problem,'

'*My* problem, my lord?'

'I was so worried that I went to your room last night. You were asleep fully clothed.'

Miss Sinclair hung her head. 'I must have been very tired. I remember having a cup of tea, and then nothing afterward.'

'Do you drink to excess?'

'No! Never!'

Her shock was very real. He studied her face. She certainly showed no physical signs of hard drinking.

'Well, to Patricia. The assemblies in Barminster are organized by a committee of local ladies—a miniature Almack's, in fact. The chief organizer is Lady Clitheroe, wife of a local squire. Now it seems that Patricia's name was neatly embroidered on the outside of her mantle. The ruffian who owns the inn where I found Patricia visited Lady Clitheroe today, brandishing the mantle and demanding to know Patricia's address, leering and saying that the young lady had gone to one of his rooms with a soldier and would no doubt pay well for his silence. He had earlier sworn to the authorities he did not know the name of the soldier. Lady Clitheroe, quite rightly, told him she would turn him over to the local magistrate for attempting to extract money with menaces. The landlord fled and the inn is now closed. It is by way of being a thieves' kitchen and the landlord has been skilful in the past at absenting himself from the town at the first sign of trouble. Why the place is not closed down...Never mind.

'The fact is that although Lady Clitheroe may not gossip with low landlords, she has a busy tongue. She arrived here just as I was finishing dinner, sighing and saying poor Patricia was ruined, and hadn't she always said such a thing would happen? It seems that before she called here, she had been gossiping about the drama to the rest of the committee. Did Patricia tell you exactly what happened?'

'Only the bare outlines. She is very defiant, I fear. She says the young man proposed to her and she saw him as a means of escape from what she describes as your tyranny. She says she did not realize how very drunk he was or she would not have encouraged him in such folly.'

'Did she tell you that when I burst into the room, the soldier was in an...er...intimate position with Patricia?'

He thought he had described it very delicately, but his description conjured up a string of erotic visions in Miss Sinclair's mind.

'No!' she gasped.

'Oh, *yes*. She must be sent away until this scandal dies down. I am travelling to town again tomorrow to seek help. I shall instruct the butler and servants that no callers are to be admitted to the house in my absence. Keep the girl busy with lessons. By God, if she were a Catholic, I would put her in a convent. Now, Miss

Sinclair, I expect you to be on your guard and to be watchful and vigilant. If any more of this heavy sleeping occurs, then I suggest you consult a physician.'

'I am sure it will not occur again,' said Miss Sinclair breathlessly.

'I would not leave her in your care had not the Lucases recommended you so highly. You may go.'

Miss Sinclair went out, feeling very downhearted. Why had she slept so heavily, so oddly? Lord Charles no longer looked at her with that mixture of respect and friendship in his eyes.

In the drawing room, Lord Charles heaved a weary sigh. It had been a long, exhausting day. He had as yet had no time to investigate the running of Burnham House or the estates. He heartily wished Patricia's father had shown more sense and left the girl in the care of some family, rather than to a bachelor like himself.

Lord Charles was gone for a month. He was away over Christmas.

Christmas at Burnham House was a dismal affair. Mindful of her duties, Miss Sinclair gave Patricia her lessons, surprised that the girl seemed almost to look forward to them.

Miss Sinclair was unusual in that she had been very well educated by her scholarly father. Like a lot of people with an academic turn of mind, she was able to communicate her enthusiasm for all kinds of subjects and yet lacked down-to-earth common sense.

Patricia tried to lose herself in her studies. Between worried governess and guilt-ridden pupil a certain bond was formed. Patricia began to find the idle gossip she had shared with Nanny Evans and Miss Simpkin and so enjoyed in the past was beginning to bore her. Miss Simpkin's brave championship made Patricia feel worse because Miss Simpkin insisted on trying to build Patricia's captain into a hero, whereas Patricia now knew that Captain Peter Oxford had been a drunk and feckless young man who had seen a chance at securing an heiress as a bride.

She hated Lord Charles and dreaded his return. Miss Sinclair loved Lord Charles and yet she too was afraid of his return lest sending Patricia away meant the end of her employment.

And then one bitter cold day he arrived.

He summoned them both to the library and told them to sit down. He looked more at ease. He looked like a man with a great weight taken off his mind.

'I have been deciding where to send you, Patricia,' he said, 'until the scandal dies down. You cannot remain cooped up here. The Lucases know of a very superior family in Boston.'

'In Boston?' said Miss Sinclair. 'Boston, *America?*'

'Yes, Boston, America. They are simple, God-fearing people with a daughter of their own. You will accompany Patricia, Miss Sinclair. She is not to return until you can write and promise me that she is become modestly behaved and fit to have a Season in London, and that there will be nothing in her manner to remind the polite world of this disgraceful episode.'

His eyes raked over Patricia's figure, which had begun to lose some of its puppy fat. 'I trust you are well in health, Patricia?'

'If you mean, am I pregnant, no!' shouted Patricia, hating him, hating him, hating him. To be sent away to the other side of the world to a country that she vaguely thought of as being full of savage

Indians and Puritans who burned witches at the stake!

'There is a ship sailing from Bristol in two weeks' time,' said Lord Charles. 'Prepare to be on it. Go to your room, Patricia. Miss Sinclair, remain. We shall discuss money arrangements.'

Patricia opened her mouth to scream that she would not go. He could not do this. This was *her* home and he was turning her out of it.

But his face was hard and implacable, all the relaxed ease of manner he had had when they entered the library completely gone.

She felt small and helpless. She turned and ran from the room.

One day she would make him pay. One day she would return and be revenged on him.

Somehow, sometime, somewhere, she would bring the haughty, bullying, satanic Lord Charles Gaunt to his knees!

FOUR

'... This town, the capital not only of Massachusetts but of all New England, is situated on a peninsula communicating with the mainland by a narrow neck upward of a mile long, which is all paved. The town of Boston is said to be about as large as New York and just as compact and the streets as irregular; the most conspicuous public buildings are the town house, in which the general court sits, and Faneuil Hall where public meetings are held. On the west of the town is Beacon Hill, a very high eminence which commands a most delightful prospect of the harbour on the south, which is interspersed with a great number of islands, among which is that whereon the castle stands.

'Mr and Mrs Munroe are all that is kind, and their daughter, Margaret, is now a close friend of Patricia. Patricia has adapted to the quieter and more staid manners of this town and is appropriately subdued in her dress, since it is not all the thing to appear aristocratic for fear of waking the never very long dormant hatred against the English...'

'What a geography lesson,' said Lord Charles, putting down Miss Sinclair's letter. 'You must excuse me for reading my post in front of you, Miss Chalmers. I always fear to learn my wayward ward has created another scandal.'

'Your concern does you credit,' said Miss Mary Chalmers.'

Lord Charles looked at her with approval.

Six months had passed since the departure of Patricia. He had found her estates as well managed as he had first thought. He had travelled to his own estates to put things in order, and then had gone south to London to visit various friends. It was at the home of Mr and Mrs George Lucas that he had first met Mary Chalmers.

Haunted as he still was by Patricia's turbulence, he found Mary Chalmers very refreshing. He thought she was like a Byzantine madonna, with her full eyes with their heavy curved lids, her thin white face, and her small curved mouth. She had a great air of repose. She never made a flurried movement or gave way to any vulgar animation.

Her father was dead and her mother was a wealthy widow. Miss Chalmers was, Lord Charles judged, about twenty-five. He wondered why she had remained unmarried for so long and then decided she was as hard to please as he was himself.

He had been invited to call and was happily drinking tea in the Chalmers' drawing room. The room was neat and cool and well ordered. No jumble of novels spilled over the table, no fashion magazines lay in untidy heaps, no feminine laces or frills hung out of the edges of workbaskets. The fire crackled, the clocks ticked, the highly polished furniture mirrored the painted ceiling. The silver, brass, and china candlesticks, fire irons, coal scuttle, cake plate, tea pot, and milk jug were all refreshingly functional. Here were no frippery Dresden shepherdesses or colourful masses of hothouse flowers.

Miss Chalmers wore no cosmetics on her pale face. Her gown was of a dull purple trimmed with black, for she was in half-mourning, her father having died two years before. More frivolous spirits might consider it a very long time to wear mourning, but Lord Charles thought it showed a womanly respect for the dead.

He had a sudden vision of Patricia, all blazing dark eyes, pink cheeks, flamboyant jewellery, alternating between tantrums and smiles.

He felt a queer little pang as he thought of a Patricia rendered dull and correct by the worthies of Boston, and quickly dismissed the picture as nonsense. His six sisters, now comfortably installed in households throughout England, had all been noisy and flighty, and all of them had settled down to become model wives. All Patricia needed to school her was a husband.

But he had never lost his temper with any of his sisters the way he had with Patricia, his conscience reminded him. Of course, his sisters had not been so terribly spoiled, and for all their faults they were ladies, and would never have ended up in a sleazy inn messing around with the breeches of some drunk in a scarlet coat. What *had* she been doing? Lord Charles thought of several very unladylike things and closed his eyes.

'I am fatiguing you, my lord,' came Miss Chalmers' calm voice. He realized she had been speaking while he was worrying about Patricia.

'I am sorry,' he said. 'You were saying...?'

'I was merely asking whether you intended to move to Brighton, Lord Charles. Mama and I have rented a house on the Steyne. London is become uncomfortably hot.'

'I have not made any plans,' he said. 'Perhaps I may visit you. I feel the need of fresh air.'

Miss Chalmers gave a little smile and looked at her hands, which were folded in her lap. Mrs Chalmers beamed at her daughter and Lord Charles. She wondered how long it would be now before his lordship proposed.

Mr and Mrs Munroe were a quiet, middle-aged couple who had arrived in Boston long after the aftermath of the Revolution when anti-English feeling still ran high. They had independent means and a thirst for travel. They had originally planned to stay in Boston only for two weeks before moving on to see New York. But they had fallen in love with the quiet town, and so they stayed. Margaret was their eldest, a girl of nineteen. They had four young sons, all still at school—which was a mercy, as Mrs Munroe pointed out to her husband, considering the devastating effect that Patricia Patterson had on all the men of the town.

Mr Munroe said placidly that the wonderful thing was that Patricia was completely unaware of her beauty or of the effect it had on any man who set eyes on her.

This was not true.

Two more years had passed since Lord Charles had sat with Mary Chalmers, thinking of Patricia. She had lost her puppy fat and had grown two inches. Her stylish clothes, all of which she made herself, were the rage of Boston.

She had a close friend in Margaret, an easy-going brunette with the same undemanding temperament as her parents. Patricia loved the whole family, and the Munroes loved her, often feeling Lord Charles was a hard guardian, for they saw nothing of the wild and wanton Patricia they had been told to expect.

Patricia had just celebrated her nineteenth birthday. Although now well beyond the age of the schoolroom, she continued to study for her own pleasure, while Miss Sinclair transferred her skills to helping the young Munroe boys who had been experiencing some difficulty with their school lessons and needed extra help.

There were many attractive men about, but Patricia cared for none. All she cared about was their reaction to her. She did not gossip or flirt, but she had an increasing feeling of power.

During her long exile, she dreamed of nothing but revenge on Lord Charles. To a sixteen-year-old, he had seemed ancient. To a now mature nineteen-year-old, he began to appear as a man who might be attracted by her beauty. That was why she took careful note of her effect on men. She never exercised any of her power over men, always turning them down, with kindness and grace, when their attentions grew too persistent.

Slowly, she began to wonder if she could possibly make Lord Charles fall in love with her.

That was the one way in which she, weaker physically, could bring him to his knees.

Behind her calm, smiling exterior, she often saw him begging, pleading for her love while she laughed in his face.

Mr and Mrs Munroe had no idea what was going on behind Patricia's pretty face. She never discussed her guardian with them. But she *had* talked about him to Margaret, and Margaret never tired of hearing stories about this wicked aristocrat, her American mind imagining a painted, bejewelled lord, lashing his tenants with a horsewhip and turning women and children out into the snow.

Miss Sinclair always praised Lord Charles, but Margaret thought Miss Sinclair a poor old maid who would naturally see no wrong in an employer since it wasn't in her interests to find any fault.

Patricia would have been very surprised if she had known how long and how often her staid governess dreamed of Lord Charles. Miss Sinclair yearned to return to England. She sent letter after letter praising Patricia's new manner, saying she had grown in charm and grace and learning and that it was surely now time for her to return and think about her first Season.

Lord Charles's replies were always courteous, but very short. He was grateful to Miss Sinclair for her regular bulletins. He was glad to hear of Patricia's improvement, but she was still young. No need to consider returning yet.

And then Miss Sinclair wrote to say she sincerely hoped she and Patricia were not trespassing on the Munroe family's hospitality too long.

At last, the letter she had been waiting and praying for arrived. Set sail as soon as possible. Patricia was to have her come-out. When they arrived at Bristol, Lord Charles wrote, the ship's agent would see them safely quartered until he, Lord Charles, was informed of their arrival and could arrange to have them met and escorted to London where they would stay at his town house.

Tears of relief poured down Miss Sinclair's face. She turned over every word Lord Charles had ever said to her, remembered his every expression, more sure than ever that he had been deeply attracted to her and yet had stopped himself from betraying that attraction because of worry about his ward.

Patricia's feelings when she received the news were mixed. Now her plan of revenge could be put into operation. But there was her regret at leaving the Munroes and their comfortable house which smelled so

American, a mixture of scented bayberry candles, apples, cornbread, and beeswax.

As they sat around the Franklin stove in the family drawing room that evening, excitedly making plans to book a passage to England, Mr Munroe wished he had written to Lord Charles suggesting Patricia should stay with them and perhaps marry a Bostonian. He had become very fond of his pretty guest. Lord Charles had sent him a letter as well, apologizing for having allowed his ward to stay so long.

Mr Munroe contented himself with begging Patricia to visit Boston again, to consider his home hers, and Patricia blinked back tears from her eyes, black thoughts of revenge seeming out of place in the midst of his happy family.

She was furious at being ordered to go to London immediately on her return. She longed to see her home again, to see Burnham House. On the other hand, it appeared Lord Charles was to be in London, and where Lord Charles was, Patricia meant to be.

Patricia and Miss Sinclair set sail in the teeth of a savage winter gale, neither particularly noticing the heaving and bucketing of the ship which was prostrating the other passengers. Miss Sinclair was going home to her love. Patricia was returning for the reckoning.

From the captain to the cabin boy, the crew were all in love with Patricia by the time the ship docked at Bristol. Miss Sinclair was delighted with her charge. Such modesty of bearing, such complete unawareness of the attention and adoration she attracted! Lord Charles would be so proud of her, the 'her' being Miss Sinclair.

'I have molded her to my image,' said Miss Sinclair, studying her face in the glass in her tiny cabin preparatory to going ashore and seeing, not really herself, but an older version of Patricia, set to take London by storm.

When they disembarked, the ship's agent met them on the quay and told them he had rooms reserved for them at the best hotel in Bristol. Word would be sent immediately to Lord Charles that they had arrived in England.

Patricia and Miss Sinclair settled down to wait, going for sedate walks about the town, each wondering, for different reasons, what Lord Charles would say when he saw them.

But, at the end of the week, it was not

Lord Charles who arrived to escort them to London, but a soberly-dressed gentleman who introduced himself as Lord Charles's secretary, Mr Johnson. And behind Mr Johnson, twittering with excitement, came none other than Miss Simpkin.

Miss Simpkin immediately launched into a long speech about *dear* Lord Charles and how he had given her permission to travel to Bristol to meet her darling Patricia, and how he had graciously said that she might stay at his town house in London to witness Patricia's debut.

Patricia was taken aback at the appearance of her old governess. Had Miss Simpkin *always* been so rouged and painted and gushing?

She supposed, after some reflection, that she had. But, nonetheless, Miss Simpkin's appearance and manner came as a shock after what seemed a lifetime with the sober Bostonians and the correct instruction of Miss Sinclair.

Patricia found herself quite out of charity with Miss Simpkin as that lady prattled on about the sterling merits of Lord Charles. But she did not contradict her. Patricia meant to lay siege to Lord Charles's flinty heart and was therefore determined to say no word of blame behind his back.

Only Margaret Munroe in Boston now knew of the depth of Patricia's hatred for her guardian.

Miss Simpkin grew increasingly disappointed in Patricia on the journey to London. In vain did she point out, at posting houses on the way to London, all the various gentlemen who were struck by her former pupil's beauty. Patricia only smiled vaguely and changed the subject.

At long last, after three days' journey, the outskirts of London began to appear and the coach rumbled and rattled over the cobbles.

Mr Johnson was a pleasant, sensible man and had passed the journey for Patricia by telling her tales of the newly-appointed Regent and the fury of the Whigs because the Prince had swung about and favoured the Tories.

It was expected to be the most glittering Season London had seen in years. The fighting was still going on in Portugal. Mr Johnson found it very shocking that some of the Whigs favoured Napoleon and thought Britain would be better under his rule than that of their own government.

Miss Sinclair was barely aware of Mr

Johnson. She was wrapped in dreams of Lord Charles and what he would say when he saw her again.

'Is Lord Charles waiting for us?' she asked.

'He will not know exactly when we are due to arrive,' said Mr Johnson. 'But his servants will know where he is and will send word to him as soon as we appear.'

Patricia's heart began to hammer as the carriage moved through the quiet streets and squares of London's West End. Lord Charles lived in Cavendish Square on the north side of Oxford Street.

'Here we are at last,' said Mr Johnson cheerfully. 'Yes, my lord must be at home and entertaining guests. There are several carriages drawn up outside.'

Patricia drew out a steel pocket mirror and anxiously pushed a stray curl back into place. Miss Simpkin smiled at this evidence of returning vanity.

The house was tall and imposing, with a pillared entrance and a double front.

The groom ran up the steps and hammered on the knocker. A butler opened the door and then stood aside to let the ladies past.

'My lord is in the library,' he said.

'Please wait one moment.'

Mr Johnson murmured that he had urgent business to attend to and vanished through a doorway at the far end of the hall.

Patricia handed the butler her card, turned down at one corner to show she was presenting it in person.

The hall was floored with black and white tiles. A huge crystal chandelier hung from the high ceiling. The walls were painted Wedgewood blue and a fire burned in the Adam fireplace. They were enclosed in the quiet well-ordered hush that only great wealth can provide.

The butler came back. 'My lord presents his compliments to Miss Patterson and desires Miss Patterson and party to present themselves in the library.'

He turned and led the way without waiting to hear their reply. Obviously, no one ever refused an invitation from Lord Charles, thought Patricia.

The butler flung open the double doors of the library. 'Miss Patricia Patterson,' he announced. Neither Miss Simpkin nor Miss Sinclair was to be honoured with an announcement. Miss Sinclair felt uneasy. She was dressed in her smartest gown and mantle. She felt that she looked every inch the lady. Why had the butler immediately assumed she was an inferior? And so Miss Sinclair fretted, not knowing that the butler had already been told to expect Miss Patterson accompanied by two governesses.

There was a lady sitting on a sofa in front of the fire with an older lady sitting beside her. There was a couple on another sofa.

Lord Charles was standing in front of the fireplace.

He and his ward stared at each other in amazement.

Patricia saw not the black-browed tyrant of her hate-filled dreams, but a tall, elegant, handsome man with thick black hair and very green eyes. His chin was strong and square and his mouth was firm. He was wearing skin-tight stockinette breeches with Hessian boots and a bottle green coat.

Lord Charles saw a very beautiful young woman, the most beautiful he had ever seen, standing in the doorway surveying him coolly. She was wearing a cherry red cloak lined with chinchilla. Her strawberry blonde curls peeped out from beneath a dashing black broad-brimmed hat trimmed with cherry red ribbons.

He walked forward and bent over Patricia's hand. His lips only brushed her glove, but they seemed to burn through the fabric.

'Patricia,' he said in a wondering voice. Green eyes met brown eyes and there was a long silence in the room as the pair stood transfixed, Lord Charles still holding Patricia's hand.

Lord Charles suddenly seemed to collect himself.

'Let me introduce you to my guests, Patricia,' he said. 'Then I am sure you will wish to retire to your room and rest. Mr and Mrs George Lucas...' Mr Lucas rose and bowed, his eyes twinkling with amusement. 'So this is Charles's little ward,' he said. 'Mrs Lucas...' Amy Lucas extended her hand and said, 'How d'you do?' in a faint voice.

'And Mrs Chalmers...' A plump, grey-haired lady looked at Patricia with cold, cold eyes. 'Humph!' she said, extending two fingers for Patricia to shake.

Patricia smiled sweetly, grabbed the startled lady's whole hand, and squeezed it in a painful grip.

'At last, but not least, Miss Chalmers...my fiancée.'

Behind Patricia, Miss Sinclair let out a sound which sounded like something between a gasp and a moan.

For one split second all expression was wiped from Patricia's face as her mind first registered, *'Married!'* But then a mocking voice in her head said, 'But not yet. Only engaged. Not yet!'

'My *dear* Miss Chalmers,' cried Patricia, sinking down onto the sofa in the space between Mary Chalmers and her mother. 'What a delightful surprise. When was the engagement announced?'

'Just last week,' said Miss Chalmers.

'Miss Chalmers is only recently out of mourning,' smiled Lord Charles. 'We had to wait until then before putting the announcement in the newspapers.'

'I am so sorry you have suffered a loss,' said Patricia. 'Your...?'

'Father. He died almost five years ago.'

'Five...!' For a moment Lord Charles thought he saw a gleam of mockery in the pansy brown eyes that turned up to briefly meet his own. 'You must have loved him very much,' added Patricia with such warm sympathy in her voice that Lord Charles was sure he must have been mistaken.

'Oh, yes,' said Miss Chalmers calmly. 'I do not approve of persons who only observe one year of mourning. It has always struck me as indecent, and dear Lord Charles agrees with me.'

'He *does?* I mean, of *course* he does,' said Patricia sweetly. 'But you still wear mourning,' she said, looking at Miss Chalmers' gown of dull grey, edged with black.

'I do not believe in wasting money on new clothes when the clothes that one has are by no means worn out,' said Miss Chalmers.

'This is very romantic,' said Patricia. 'What a wonderful homecoming. You must be the envy of every lady of the ton, Miss Chalmers, to have captured my so very dashing and handsome guardian.'

She turned and smiled at Lord Charles, a dazzling, bewitching smile, and Lord Charles smiled back, blinking a little as if blinded by the light.

The battle for Lord Charles's heart had begun in earnest.

FIVE

There was a little silence when Patricia, Miss Simpkin, and Miss Sinclair finally left the room.

'What a dasher!' exclaimed George Lucas. 'You will have no trouble at all in marrying her off. They'll be beating a path to your door, old boy.'

'She is exquisite,' said his wife, still looking dazed. 'Not only her beauty, but the elegance of her manners and dress.'

'I gather Miss Sinclair has done a magnificent job,' said Mary Chalmers. 'I feel you are to be reproved, Lord Charles. You did not address one word to that estimable creature. She seemed to me to be a very superior sort of person.'

'You are right,' said Lord Charles ruefully. 'I will speak to her later. I confess, I am still taken aback at the change in Patricia.'

'Too good-looking for her own good,' snorted Mrs Chalmers. 'Those sort of looks don't last, mark my words. What a gel needs is an air of good breeding.' She pressed her daughter's hand fondly.

Lord Charles looked down at Mrs Chalmers with a certain amount of irritation. He wondered if he would ever be allowed to see Mary alone, even after they were wed. Mrs Chalmers was always present, and he felt sure Mary would have married him long ago if her mother had not been intent on fostering this unnaturally prolonged mourning for a man long dead.

Lord Charles sometimes felt the strain of being obliged to conduct himself with decorum on all occasions.

The Lucases had accepted his engagement philosophically, Mrs Lucas saying wryly that he was obviously determined to marry someone who would not cause him one day's upset.

And Lord Charles, thinking of his sisters, craved peace and quiet in his home. It had been a stormy time, steering them clear of unsuitable men and fortune hunters. He remembered the scenes when Amy, the youngest, had declared herself to be passionately in love with the second footman. Lord Charles had been immensely relieved to find out that her declaration had come as much as a surprise to the second footman as it had to himself.

Now there was one last hurdle—Patricia. With any luck she would be engaged before the month was out. Then he could marry Mary Chalmers and retire to his estates in the country and sink into tranquil middle age, surrounded by his children.

A frown creased his brow. Children. Would Mary...? *Could* Mary...? When he had proposed to her, the one time Mrs Chalmers had left them alone, and she had accepted him, he had taken her in his arms and kissed her. The fact that he had felt absolutely no stirring of the senses had not surprised him at the time. He was engaged to a lady, and well-bred ladies did not excite passion. Now he felt a little stabbing pang of disappointment.

For the first time he began to wonder about his own behaviour, and why he had patiently waited so long to claim the hand of a woman who appeared to enjoy her mourning state and who was reluctant to give it up.

The disloyalty of his thoughts shocked him almost as soon as they were formed.

There was no doubt about it—Miss Patricia Patterson was a disruptive influence.

The disruptive influence had taken off her bonnet upstairs and was looking with pleasure about the sunny room allocated to her. In Boston, she had shared a bedroom with Margaret. It was lovely to have a room of her own again.

As chambermaids unpacked her trunks, she sat down by the window and looked out on London.

Lord Charles was an attractive man, and it would not be easy to entrap him. The challenge made Patricia tingle with excitement. She had never really put her charms to the test. The first thing she would have to do would be to see if she could make him jealous.

The need to confide in someone was great. She crossed to an escritoire in the corner and pulled forward a clean sheet of paper, dipped the pen in the inkwell, and began to write.

'Dear Margaret...'

After Miss Chalmers and her mother and the Lucases had left, Lord Charles sent for Miss Sinclair.

She arrived, looking tired and depressed. His engagement had been a sad blow to her dreams.

'Sit down, Miss Sinclair,' said Lord Charles in a kind voice. 'I shall not keep you long. You must be fatigued after your long journey.'

'No, not at all,' she said, looking at him longingly. 'Mr Johnson was all that is kind and looked after our every comfort.'

'He is a good man and an excellent secretary. I wish to compliment you on the change in Patricia. You have done your work well, Miss Sinclair. I am grateful to you. I do not think it will be long before she is married, and then your duties will cease. To show you how grateful I am, I wish to give you a sum of money and to arrange a pension for you so that you may be a lady of independent means, and ensure that you will not be obliged to seek another position unless you so wish.'

'You are very kind,' said Miss Sinclair with very real gratitude. 'But it is only to be expected. You are so fine, so noble—'

'Enough, Miss Sinclair. Spare my blushes. Mr Johnson will settle all the details. You may go. Patricia will no doubt receive many invitations. I would be obliged if you would act as chaperone.'

'Gladly, my lord.'

'Then that will be all, Miss Sinclair.'

He smiled at her again and hope sprang anew in Miss Sinclair's bosom.

'My lord, accept my congratulations on your forthcoming marriage.'

'Thank you.'

'Miss Chalmers appears an estimable lady, and yet she is undoubtedly fortunate.'

There was something in the yearning warmth of Miss Sinclair's voice that set alarm bells ringing in his lordship's head.

He looked at her fully for the first time. Her eyes were glowing and her cheeks were stained with pink. Her bosom was heaving and her lips trembled.

'I consider myself a lucky man,' said Lord Charles evenly. 'Miss Chalmers is everything I desire in a wife. I trust she, too, can count on your loyalty and devotion.'

Lost hope erased the colour and glow from Miss Sinclair's face as if a sponge had been wiped across it.

'Of course, my lord.'

He looked at her calmly, politely, waiting for her to leave.

Miss Sinclair trailed from the room.

The door closed behind her, softly.

'Oh, dear,' said Lord Charles Gaunt.

Patricia was disappointed to find she was not to see Lord Charles for the rest of that day. He had gone to the opera with Miss Chalmers and her mother.

On the following day, by the time she made her way downstairs, it was to find he had gone riding in the Park. He did not return until six that evening, when he smiled at her in a vague way and said he was going to his club.

'I thought I was to make my come-out, my lord,' said Patricia tartly. 'Not my stay-in.'

'I am taking you to the ball tomorrow,' he said, pulling on his gloves. 'Did I not tell you?'

'No, I had begun to think you had forgotten me.' How large and dark her eyes looked, and how wistful.

'On the contrary, I have been as busy as any matchmaking mama on your behalf. We have many invitations. They are all addressed to me, but include you. Ask Mr Johnson to let you see them. If there are any you do not wish to attend, please let him know,'

'Oh, I wish to attend them *all*,' said Patricia. 'I shall dance and dance.' She pirouetted about the hall, her skirts flying, the very picture of youth and grace.

He tried to think of her as little more than a child, but found his eyes straying to the trimness of her ankles revealed by the swaying of her skirt.

'Good evening,' he said gruffly, almost harshly.

Patricia watched him as he strode away, a little smile curling her lips. Then she turned and ran up the stairs to look out her most dazzling ballgown, one she had made herself but not dared wear in Boston for fear of being damned as 'aristocratic.'

Patricia put it on and surveyed herself in the mirror.

The glory of the gown lay in the intricate embroidery of the overdress. Margaret and Patricia had discovered a talented young Frenchman in Boston who was able to make paste jewellery which looked real. Patricia had bought many fake gems from him and had woven an intricate pattern ornamented with paste diamonds and rubies onto two broad silk bands of embroidery down the front of the white gauze overdress. The thickly encrusted embroidery depicted flowers and leaves in a Jacobean pattern. The underdress was a simple sheath of white silk.

Her silk slippers were ruby red and her headdress was a circlet of red silk flowers with a 'ruby' in the centre of each one.

She had let her hair grow long and the ruby red of her silk flowers, instead of detracting from the colour of her hair, enhanced it.

On a girl of lesser beauty, the whole ensemble might have looked vulgar. On Patricia, it looked magnificent.

The following evening when Patricia entered the drawing room Lord Charles felt his breath catch in his throat.

She blazed with beauty, like her gems. Her eyes were large and dark and sparkling in the perfect oval of her face.

Then his face hardened. He had allowed Patricia a generous allowance during her stay in Boston, but that allowance surely did not stretch to the payment of jewel-encusted Paris gowns.

'Who paid for all this magnificence?' he demanded.

'I did,' said Patricia. 'Do you not like it?'

'On the allowance I sent you, you could not possibly afford so many jewels. You are wearing a king's ransom!'

'I made the gown myself,' said Patricia.

'The jewels are paste. Oh, I should have known you would spoil my evening. I thought you would have been proud of my skill.'

Her large eyes filled with tears.

'My dear Patricia,' said Lord Charles, horrified. 'I did not know...the jewels look so real...please do not cry.'

But Patricia subsided gracefully on to a sofa and, shaking out a wisp of a handkerchief, applied it to her eyes.

'I must admit, I do consider Patricia's gown entirely unsuitable for a debut,' said Miss Sinclair. 'Simple white would be best. Patricia has some very pretty gowns...'

'She will do very well,' said Lord Charles. He reached down, took Patricia's hand holding the handkerchief, and drew it gently away from her suspiciously dry eyes.

She quickly dropped her lids, her thick lashes fanning across her cheeks.

'Come now,' he said gently. 'Miss Chalmers is waiting for us.'

Eyes still downcast, Patricia rose to her feet. He held out his arm, looking down at her sharply, suddenly sure she was laughing at him. But she raised her eyes to him and said simply, 'Thank you,

113

my lord,' and took his arm. He felt absurdly large and protective. He paused in the hall and took Patricia's cloak from Miss Sinclair and put it about his ward's shoulders.

Patricia was wearing a light flowery scent. He wondered what it was. He smiled down at her as he escorted her out to his carriage. Miss Sinclair wished bitterly Lord Charles would smile at *her* in that caressing way, and the first seed of envy of her beautiful charge was planted in Miss Sinclair's bosom.

She was not to be alone in her envy. Mrs Chalmers and her daughter did not see the full glory that was Patricia until they arrived at the ball, since Patricia had been shrouded in her cloak. It was only when they were removing their wraps in the anteroom at the Earl and Countess of Strathairn's London home that the full glittering effect of Patricia's ensemble burst before their eyes.

Miss Chalmers put a restraining hand on Patricia's arm as she was about to leave the anteroom. 'My dear Miss Patterson,' she said, 'I can see you are not quite *au fait* with our London ways. Modest attire is deemed suitable for any young lady making her come-out. Your gown will draw too much attention to you.'

'It will?' said Patricia sweetly. 'Oh, *good!*' And with that she walked past Miss Chalmers and out into the hall where Lord Charles was waiting for them.

Mary Chalmers rounded on Miss Sinclair. 'I would have thought *you*, as a woman of sense, would have advised your charge better,' she said.

'I tried to say something,' said Miss Sinclair, 'but Lord Charles did not pay any attention. I am surprised. When we were in Boston, Patricia was a model of propriety.'

'I shall speak to you further on this matter,' said Miss Chalmers. 'The gentlemen do not notice such nuances of fashion. But she will disgrace poor Charles!'

They, too, went forward to join Lord Charles.

Miss Chalmers was wearing dove grey silk edged with purple ribbon. Her gown had a modest neckline and long, tight sleeves.

Lord Charles found himself wondering with a certain amount of irritation whether his beloved meant to get *married* in half mourning. Again, he blamed Mrs Chalmers.

But Mary's fondness for mourning had little to do with her mother. Mrs Chalmers was beginning to get worried. Her poor moth of a Mary was completely outshone by the dazzling butterfly that was Patricia Patterson.

She had begged Mary to encourage a proposal from Lord Charles a long time earlier, saying that if she did not snap him up, someone else would. But Mary had a solid core of vanity and was very sure of Lord Charles. It suited her very well to be courted. She enjoyed her single state and did not wish to hurry into marriage. She had been courted before, many times, because she was a wealthy heiress, but had always considered that her attraction lay in her well-bred and ladylike appearance. The fact that girls much prettier than herself were still unwed, she put down to their vulgar, pushing ways, not noticing that the unwed girls she so pitied had very little in the way of a dowry.

Love and beauty did not play much part in the Marriage Mart. Marriage was a way of increasing one's land and fortune. But Mary Chalmers, despite the fact that she prided herself on being knowledgeable about the ways of the ton, refused to grasp these simple facts, and had come to think herself irresistible.

She had never needed to feel possessive about Lord Charles before this evening. He had dutifully danced with other ladies, but had always returned to her side with a sigh of relief.

But tonight his pride in his beautiful ward was there for all to see.

Patricia was mobbed. The gentlemen all swore she was the most beautiful thing they'd ever seen, and the ladies set out to woo Miss Sinclair to try to discover the name of Patricia's dressmaker.

Loyalty to Lord Charles rather than loyalty to Patricia had kept Miss Sinclair from telling anyone that Patricia made her gown herself.

Lord Charles danced twice with Patricia, which was to be expected. But at the end of the evening when he stood up with her for a third time, eyebrows started to raise. Lord Charles knew he was causing gossip, but for once he did not care. Patricia was his ward. It was his duty to look after her. She flirted with him and teased him and he felt light-hearted and amused and much younger than he had felt since his mother had died and saddled him with the worries of bringing six sisters up and 'out.' His older brother, the heir, had been no help, being taken up with the cares of the estate.

When they were promenading after their third dance, he looked down at her, his green eyes glinting, and said, 'Now, look what you have made me do. Three dances. I shall never hear the end of it.'

'Pooh! You are my stuffy old guardian,' laughed Patricia. 'And you are happily engaged to a sterling lady. In fact, you are the most respectable person at this ball.'

His thin brows snapped together in annoyance, and she added lightly, 'But you are also the handsomest man in the room.'

His face lightened. 'You are a terrible flirt, Patricia. What of Mr Brummell over there?'

'Well, he is very clean. He is the most *polished* man I have ever seen. His face glows like a sunrise.'

Lord Charles laughed appreciatively. The famous Beau Brummell had a habit of scrubbing his face with a flesh-brush until he looked 'very much like a man in the scarlet fever.' The result was actually a salmon-coloured glow. He was not content with merely shaving, but went over his face with eyebrow tweezers afterward to make absolutely sure that no stray whisker marred his face. His morning toilet took as long as five hours: two hours bathing in water, milk, and eau de cologne, a further hour inching himself into skin-tight buckskin breeches, another hour with his hairdresser, and a final hour discarding as many as a dozen cravats before he was satisfied with the result.

'At least we must be grateful to the Beau for having introduced clean linen and plenty of washing to the ton,' said Lord Charles. 'Many of them are still in need of it. Now, *you* smell exactly like a bouquet of freshly-picked garden flowers. What is the name of your scent?'

'I haven't given it one yet,' said Patricia. 'I made it myself in Boston and brought some bottles back with me.'

'There is no end to your talents.'

'Perhaps,' said Patricia, flirting with her fan. 'Perhaps I have some hidden talents, not yet tried.'

'Such as?'

'Making love.'

'Fie for shame, Patricia Patterson! That

is the remark of a member of the demimonde.'

'You interest me. Do ladies *never* make love?'

'Never. They are made love *to.*'

'How boring,' said Patricia lightly. 'I must search around for a gentleman who does not hold such stuffy ideas. All my heroes cannot be in books.'

'You will find they are, and *better* where they are. Or do you dream of some Lochinvar who will ride out of the West to sweep you away?'

'Of course.'

'Then you will never make a suitable marriage,' he said, suddenly serious. 'I had hoped you had grown out of such fantasies. Only look where such nonsense led you when you were sixteen.'

'You are cruel to remind me of that. I wonder where the dear captain is now?'

'You are incorrigible.'

'No, simply young and happy and determined not to die an old maid. Oh, do look at Miss Chalmers. You have neglected her sorely.'

'You are right. And here is your next partner.' He bowed and left her and went quickly to join Mary.

'I have had little opportunity to speak to you this evening,' she said when he sat down beside her. 'I am very shocked at Miss Patterson's outlandish gown.'

'It *is* unconventional,' he agreed. 'But, by George, she knows how to wear it, and what is more, get away with wearing it.'

Mary smoothed down the silk of her gown. 'Dazzling, I agree, but then it will attract the wrong sort of man. Any man who admires that showy style is not *au fond* a gentleman.'

He was irritated by her remarks, but, nonetheless, had come to rely on her wisdom.

On their return to Cavendish Square in the early hours of the morning and when they were drinking tea in the drawing room, Lord Charles pointed out to Patricia that her dress had been a trifle outrageous and was bound to attract the wrong sort of gentleman.

'What an old-maidish thing to say,' laughed Patricia. 'Never mind. I planned to cut a dash on my first evening. Everything I wear from now on would not even raise an eyebrow in Boston.'

She rose gracefully to her feet.

'Hey ho, how weary I am of lectures.

121

What a bear you are, my wicked guardian. I shall leave you to your evil thoughts.'

She stood on tiptoe and kissed him lightly on the cheek, and then turned and tripped from the room. Miss Sinclair rushed after her, and soon Lord Charles could hear the governess's voice, scolding Patricia for being so forward all the way up the stairs.

Lord Charles's hand strayed to his cheek where she had kissed him. Perhaps he would take her driving in the afternoon and introduce her to some suitable gentlemen.

But surely he had said something about calling on Mary. He gave a little shrug. It was his duty to concentrate on Patricia. After all, he was going to *marry* Mary.

It was sunny in the Park, the dust from the wheels of the many carriages rising in the air, making the multi-coloured scene look like a tapestry.

Patricia sat up beside Lord Charles in his high-perch phaeton, wearing a dashing straw hat, the underside of the brim ornamented with a whole garden of flowers. Her gown and pelisse were of palest yellow muslin and she carried a lace and gauze yellow parasol. She was highly amused and not at all impressed by the various dandies she saw on the strut. 'They look like wasps,' she said, 'with their puffed-out chests and nipped-in waists and striped waistcoats. That gentleman over there has such high heels on his boots he can hardly walk!'

'You must not laugh so openly at them,' warned Lord Charles. 'They can be malicious.'

She looked at him curiously, at the elegance of his clothes and the strength of his legs in their leather breeches, and asked, 'And what are you, my lord? Dandy or Corinthian, Choice Spirit, Fop, Pink of the Ton, or Buck?'

'I am myself,' he said. 'I have never tried to set the fashion.'

'And yet you do!' exclaimed Patricia. 'Several gentlemen I danced with last night were more interested in the name of your tailor than they were in any of my charms. I was quite cast down, I assure you.'

'A little casting down might be good for you, Patricia. You are too ebullient. One is not supposed to appear to *enjoy* the Season.'

'I should behave like this?' Patricia leaned back in the carriage and adopted an air of petulant world-weariness.

'Something like that,' he laughed. 'Are you enjoying your drive?'

'I always enjoy being with you,' she said in a casual voice, and he looked at her sharply.

'I am flattered,' he said. 'I thought you considered me to be as old as Methuselah.'

'That was when I was sixteen. Now I am older and more mature, I think you are quite the right age.'

'For what?'

'I cannot possibly answer that. You are affianced to Miss Chalmers.'

'That cannot possibly prevent you from answering my question.'

'You are being deliberately obtuse,' said Patricia. 'You know *exactly* what I mean.'

He felt a dangerous, heady excitement as if he were slightly drunk. To change the subject, he said, 'Is there anything else in London you would like to see?'

'All the unfashionable places,' said Patricia. 'I would like to see the wild beasts at the Tower.'

'Very well.' He neatly turned his carriage about and started to drive smartly toward the gates of Hyde Park.

'Never say you are taking me there,' said

Patricia. 'The great Lord Charles behaving like the veriest yokel. People will say I have bewitched you.'

'How could they say such nonsense when all the world already knows I have been bewitched by Miss Chalmers?'

Patricia tilted her parasol to hide her face. She did not believe for one moment he was in love with Mary Chalmers. One had only to see them together. Patricia's conscience gave her a sharp stab. It was really rather a dirty trick to try to woo Miss Chalmer's fiancé away from her—unlikeable and prissy though she might be. *But I am only borrowing him,* she told herself fiercely. He is not in love with Mary, and so, after I have rejected him, he will return to her arms with a sigh of relief and their marriage will probably be happier than it would otherwise be.

'We are to go to Vauxhall tonight,' said Lord Charles, breaking into her thoughts. 'Did Mr Johnson tell you?'

'Yes,' said Patricia. 'Or rather he told Miss Sinclair, who told me.'

'You and Miss Sinclair must have become very close in Boston.'

'Not exactly,' said Patricia cautiously. 'I was very friendly with Margaret Munroe and Miss Sinclair spent most of her time instructing the young Munroe boys. She likes to teach and is a good instructress. It is a pity, however...'

Patricia bit her lip and fell silent. She had been about to add, 'It is a pity she is so silly.' But that would have been unfair. Patricia thought a great part of Miss Sinclair's silliness was caused by the governess's forming a tendre for Lord Charles. She had suspected it, but had not been sure until she had begun to notice Miss Sinclair's breathless excitement as they approached London and how often she studied her face in the glass.

'What is a pity?'

'Oh, nothing,' said Patricia vaguely. 'Who is going to be at Vauxhall?'

'There's you and Miss Sinclair, myself and Miss Chalmers—'

'And of course, Mrs Chalmers,' said Patricia wickedly.

'And, of course, Mrs Chalmers,' he said equably. 'Then there are the Lucases, and a friend of mine from my army days, Colonel Brian Sommers. Very handsome.'

'Perhaps I shall fall in love with the colonel.'

'You could do worse. He is an amiable

man and a bachelor.'

He then began to tell her about Vauxhall Pleasure Gardens on the south side of the river, describing the music and fireworks, and Patricia scowled under the shade of her parasol, feeling he was once more talking to her as if she were a child.

The Tower of London loomed up against the clear blue sky.

'Where are the animals kept?' asked Patricia.

'In the Lion Barbican. I do not know if they make an impressive spectacle. I have not visited the Tower since I was a boy.'

'Did your mother take you?'

'No, of course not. My tutor took me along once on my birthday.'

'Were you always in the care of servants when you were small?'

'I was, as is everybody.'

'Not everybody. You mean only the small world of the ton. I have observed the lower orders do not leave their children to the care of others.'

'You do not approve of servants bringing up children? Yet you seem to have been much indulged by your nanny and Miss Simpkin.'

'I was lucky. Others are not, I believe,

so fortunate. Besides, it strikes me as unnatural. If I had a baby, I would wish to caress it and sing it lullabies.'

'In my case,' he said, 'my mother was ailing for much of my childhood. When she died, my father and elder brother did not know what to do about launching my sisters into the world. Either I would have to undertake the task, or they would have been left with the servants at home. I had no desire to see them suffer. The servants were...unkind. I took the house in town, engaged an elderly aunt as chaperone, and did my best for them. An unusual arrangement, I think.'

'And they all married well?'

'Very well. They are spread throughout the country and all of them now have children of their own. They do not come to London, which is why you have not met any of them.'

'But a *man* to have charge of six girls! I suppose that was why my father decided to leave me in your care.'

'Perhaps. Or perhaps he did not know of any suitable female. Here we are.'

He jumped down and then held up his arms to help her from the carriage.

She tumbled forward so that he had

to catch hold of her tightly. For a brief moment, a delectable bosom was pressed against his chest and a beautiful, laughing face was turned up to his own. He realized to his horror he had been within an ames ace of kissing her as he quickly released her and turned sharply away.

'Has there always been a menagerie here?' asked Patricia, hurrying to keep up with his long strides.

'I think it was started in the thirteenth century by Henry III. He started off by keeping a polar bear. It was a great success until he ordered the sheriffs to pay fourpence a day for its upkeep.

'Mind you, the animal was a great favourite and crowds would flock to watch it fishing in the river. After that, Henry then instructed his sheriffs to build a house at the Tower forty feet by twenty to house his elephant. I think the original site of the menagerie must have been somewhere in the Outer Bailey. King Henry's elephant died after only two years of captivity and the elephant house was turned into a prison.

'By Edward II's reign the Keeper of the King's Lions and Leopards was a regular appointment carrying a fixed wage and lodgings within the Tower.'

They walked along beside the cages examining the dusty, ragged-looking collection of beasts. The air was hot and stifling and the smell was abominable.

'Let us go,' said Patricia miserably. 'It is not all all what I expected. Poor animals.' She had forgotten for the moment to try to charm Lord Charles, but as her eyes filled with tears, he felt a tugging at his heart and a longing to take her in his arms.

She looked so sad and forlorn as they drove off that he racked his brains for something to distract her.

'The Monument!' he said, seeing the tall pillar rising ahead of them. 'Would you like to climb up it? The view is said to be very fine.'

'Oh, yes,' said Patricia brightening.

The Momument to the great fire of London—'The loftiest stone column in the world'—rose 202 feet high above the surrounding houses. On a plaque on the side, the 'Popish faction' was blamed for starting the fire, although there was no proof of the Catholics having had anything to do with it whatsoever.

When they were about to climb up the 311 steps on the inside of the pillar, Lord

Charles hesitated. It was getting late, and he had really meant to call on Mary after that drive in the Park.

But Patricia had already started to climb, and so he followed her, determined to make his peace with Mary later.

Flushed and breathless, Patricia at last stood on the platform at the top. London lay spread out at her feet, seeming to swim in the hazy golden light of afternoon. A whole forest of masts bobbed lazily in the waters of the Thames below.

'How beautiful,' sighed Patricia.

She took off her bonnet and let it dangle by the strings. A light breeze blew a lock of hair across her face.

'Yes. Very beautiful,' said Lord Charles, his eyes on Patricia.

Without turning around, she became intensely aware of him. She felt sure she could encourage him to kiss her. But all at once she became alarmed at the intensity of her own feelings. For she wanted him to kiss her more than anything in the world. This was no way to plan revenge.

She turned her back on the shining city and walked slowly to the stairs.

'Something has upset you?' he said. His voice was deep and husky. She turned and looked up into his green eyes, seeing the concern and warmth and kindness there.

She dropped her eyes quickly. 'Nothing,' she mumbled. 'I was merely thinking of those poor animals in the Tower.'

He led the way down, feeling as if all the magic and excitement had gone out of the day. But Patricia became dizzy with all the turns of the spiral staircase and had a fit of the giggles, and soon he found himself laughing as well.

Lord Charles thought of Mary, thought of Mrs Chalmers, and wanted to delay the outing just a little longer.

On the road back he insisted on stopping at a pastry cook's. Patricia ate several cakes, laughing at him and saying he was trying to make her as fat as she had been when she was sixteen.

Then she asked him all about the long war in the Peninsula and he talked and talked as the sun sank lower in the sky and the bells of the City churches rang for evensong.

At last he pulled a heavy gold watch from his waistcoat and looked at the time in alarm. 'Eight o'clock, Patricia,' he said. 'Now I *am* in the suds. We were supposed to call at Miss Chalmer's home at seven-thirty before going to Vauxhall.'

'We shall not be so very late,' coaxed Patricia. 'I can change very quickly. Oh, do you think we might take Miss Simpkin with us? She does so enjoy some gaiety and her role has been usurped by Miss Sinclair. And no one can possibly accuse me of being fast with *two* governesses by my side.'

'You may bring Miss Simpkin. But *hurry*. We are very late. I hope you are not going to be sick. You ate so many cakes.'

'I was hungry,' laughed Patricia. 'I won't eat anything else until tomorrow.'

Miss Sinclair was pacing up and down the hall when they arrived. 'I am so glad you are safe!' she cried. 'I feared an accident. The Chalmers' footman has just left. Mrs Chalmers sent him, demanding news of you.'

'As you can see, we are both well,' said Lord Charles. 'I shall send a message to Mrs Chalmers and to my fiancée that we were delayed. Tell Miss Simpkin she is to accompany us as well. Now, Patricia, let us see how quickly you can dress!'

Patricia ran lightly up the stairs. She turned on the landing and leaned over the bannister. 'I forgot to thank you for a wonderful day,' she called softly.

'The pleasure was all mine,' laughed Lord Charles.

Miss Sinclair looked from one to the other, her back rigid with disapproval. Poor Miss Chalmers. Patricia was behaving in a disgracefully *intimate* way with Lord Charles, who, like all gentlemen, was so easily duped. That disgraceful affair with the soldier—that was obviously the real Patricia. She had merely *pretended* to be good and demure in Boston.

In her muddled way, Miss Sinclair was already making up her mind that if *she* could not have Lord Charles, then Patricia was certainly not going to. But she forced that ignoble thought far down inside and told herself righteously that it was up to her to save Lord Charles's engagement to a highly suitable lady.

This determination was strengthened when they arrived at the Chalmers' home. After Lord Charles had cheerfully—and heartlessly, Miss Sinclair thought—explained the reason for his tardiness, he then turned to Mrs Chalmers to enquire politely about her health, since Mrs Chalmers suffered from rheumatism. While they were engaged in conversation, Mary Chalmers drew Miss Sinclair a little to one side and said in a low voice, 'Was it necessary to bring that dreadful old governess along? Such a person must offend *your* sensibilities, Miss Sinclair.'

Miss Sinclair looked to where Miss Simpkin sat, sipping ratafia and beaming vaguely around, and murmured, 'Yes, indeed, but I fear Patricia must have persuaded Lord Charles to include her in the party. And to think that *I* was engaged to try to undo the harm that woman, Simpkin, had done.'

'Have you no influence with Miss Patterson?' asked Mary. 'Her manner to her guardian is very bold and forward.'

'I am afraid he encourages her,' said Miss Sinclair. 'Never fear, I will see what I can do.'

'I am sure you will,' said Mary in a low voice. 'You are very kind.'

Miss Sinclair glowed with loyalty. Here was a lady who appreciated her worth and who spoke to her as one equal to another.

But it was very hard to get near Patricia. They were joined by Lord Charles's friends, the Lucases, and with them came Colonel Brian Sommers. He was a tall and amiable gentleman with a splendid pair of flaxen military whiskers. He brightened perceptibly when he saw Patricia and promptly moved to her side as if determined to stay there for the rest of the evening.

As they set out for Vauxhall, Lord Charles took the Lucases and Mary and her mother in his carriage and Colonel Brian Sommers followed in his with Patricia and the two governesses.

With eyes sharpened with jealousy, Miss Sinclair noticed that in Lord Charles's absence, Patricia became quiet and demure again and only replied half-heartedly to the colonel's compliments.

Patricia was surprised that the staid Miss Chalmers had agreed to visit Vauxhall. Although the gardens were very pretty and hundreds of lamps hung from the trees, it was a circus of a place with dancing floors, spectacular panoramas of Artic regions, Indian jugglers, Mr Ducrow's 'equestrian entertainments,' and the 'ethereal Saqui'—a sturdy looking lady in a Roman helmet who descended the slack wire on one toe.

All classes mixed freely—too freely to judge from the giggles and squeals coming from the darker parts of the walks.

Nor were they free from the noisy crowd when they took their places in the box in the Rotunda. For the Bucks and Bloods passing underneath ogled Patricia quite dreadfully and the prostitutes tried to do business with Lord Charles, the colonel, and Mr Lucas.

Miss Sinclair's sharpened eyes noticed that Patricia was flirting with the colonel and yet glancing sideways at Lord Charles to see what he was making of it.

Lord Charles was suddenly very tired and very bored. He racked his brain for a topic of conversation but he could think of nothing. Surely he and Mary had talked amicably for hours? What had they talked about? He could not remember.

Mrs Chalmers was prosing on about her rheumatism and how she feared the air of the gardens was damp. Mary nodded and smiled her little curved smile and arranged her mother's wraps about her shoulders.

The only person who seemed to be truly and uncomplicatedly happy was Miss Simpkin, who watched the moving, shifting throng with bright eyes.

'Your ward is drinking punch,' said

137

Mary in Lord Charles's ear.

'Let her. She is old enough.'

'I do not agree with you. Patricia has become bold in her manner.'

Lord Charles looked across to where Patricia was conversing with the colonel. There was nothing vulgar in her manner that he could see.

'I can hardly check her in front of the company,' he pointed out.

'But *later*...'

'Yes, yes,' he said testily, for the colonel and Patricia had risen to their feet.

'Going to see the fireworks,' said the colonel. 'Told Miss Patterson they were worth a look.'

Lord Charles nodded and watched them go. Then he muttered with annoyance. Colonel Sommers was easy-going and absent-minded. Smitten as he obviously was with Patricia's charms, he was, nonetheless, not making a very good escort. They were being buffeted and jostled by the throng, and one drunken Buck tried to get his arm around Patricia's waist. She shrank away from him, but the colonel did not even seem to notice.

'Excuse me,' said Lord Charles hurriedly. He vaulted over the edge of the box and then started shouldering his way through the crowd.

Patricia was just about to seize hold of Colonel Sommers' arm. She turned her head and, looking back, saw Lord Charles rapidly gaining on them.

A noisy crowd of revellers pushed their way between the colonel and Patricia and she deliberately allowed herself to be swept to one side. The colonel ambled on and then looked around in bewilderment, obviously wondering where she had gone. Patricia was wearing white flowers in her hair. The colonel was a trifle short-sighted. He saw a girl with white flowers in her hair bobbing along with the crowd ahead of him, and, convinced it was Patricia, he set out in pursuit.

'Where's Brian?' asked Lord Charles, catching up with Patricia and glaring ferociously at a burly young man who had been about to speak to her.

'I've lost him,' said Patricia.

'I am not surprised. What a rabble! Let's go back.'

'I did so want to see the fireworks,' pleaded Patricia. 'The Lucases and Miss Chalmers will understand. I am still a country yokel. Please. Just this once.'

'Very well...only we cannot stay long.'

'I wonder where Charles has gone?' Mary Chalmers was saying.

'Probably to watch the fireworks,' said George Lucas rather testily. He thought Mary Chalmers a poor sort of woman. Everything she said always seemed to be tinged with disapproval. But he was fond of Lord Charles, so he added, 'I am sure my wife will excuse me if you would like me to escort you to the display, Miss Chalmers.'

'Not I,' said Mary. 'I do not like fireworks. They are extremely dangerous. Lord Charles is of the same opinion.'

'I feel like walking about a bit,' said George Lucas. 'Come along, Mrs Lucas, we'll get a bit of exercise.'

'It is very bad of Charles to stay away,' said Mrs Lucas when the couple were finally a little away from the crowds in a tree-lined walk. 'Do you think he is falling in love with his ward?'

'Not Charles,' said Mr Lucas comfortably. 'Never has been in love, and never will be. Stands to reason. If he'd had any sense, he'd have snapped *you* up. Thank goodness he didn't, or I wouldn't have stood a chance.'

'Silly,' said Mrs Lucas with a giggle. 'Still, I am very fond of Charles and I don't think we will see much of him after he is married. *She* doesn't like us.'

'*She* doesn't like anyone,' said Mr Lucas. 'I would like to see Charles with someone younger, prettier, and happier.'

'Like Patricia Patterson?'

'She *is* a charming little thing. Some scandal about her, though. Had to be sent to America.'

'Whatever it was, it could not have been so very bad or Charles would not waste so much time on her,' said Mrs Lucas. 'If only we had not invited Miss Chalmers to our house that afternoon. Charles would never have met her.'

'Why did we invite her?'

'It was my fault. I met her at the Southerns' musicale. I ripped my gown on one of their rickety chairs and Miss Chalmers proved to be very helpful with a needle and thread. So I invited her.'

'Well, who would ever think Charles would even look at her.'

Mrs Lucas sighed. 'Shall we go back and join the severe young governess and the frozen-faced Chalmerses?'

'No. Let's be very selfish and go home.

All this noise is making my head ache. One orchestra is playing one tune over there, and t'other's making a different sort of row on the other side of the walk.'

'What shall we tell Charles when we see him again?'

'Say you had the vapours.'

'I never have them, silly.'

'Bound to be a first time.'

'We'll send a boy back to the box with a message, and that way Charles will know not to wait for us.'

They walked off amicably, hand in hand, debating whether to hire a hack or to take a ferry back to the north side of the river.

Below the fireworks platform at the eastern end of the grounds, Patricia stood with her hands clasped, watching the fireworks burst against the night sky.

Lord Charles watched Patricia's upturned face.

He had often wondered since that disastrous night with the young soldier whether Patricia had retained her virginity. Now, he was sure she had. There was a freshness about her, an *untouched* air. But he had to be sure for his own peace of mind.

'Why?' he demanded suddenly. 'Why

did you run off with that soldier, and what really happened?'

His voice was low and yet Patricia heard every word. 'We cannot talk here,' she said.

'Let us move a little away,' he urged. He suddenly felt he had to know all about it immediately.

They walked back down the deserted walk. Everyone else was still watching the display.

There was a little arbour set among a stand of trees a few yards to the side of the walk. Lord Charles led her there and waited until she was seated before asking again, 'Why?'

Patricia gave a little sigh. She seemed to be looking back at another Patricia, wilful and headstrong and determined to get her own way.

'I was furious,' she said. 'I had been used to being mistress in my own house. Suddenly, the servants would only obey *your* orders. I felt I was too old to be confined to the school-room. I drank too much at the ball. I know the captain's name, but it doesn't matter now. *He* was deathly drunk. I only realized that afterward. At the time he seemed young and carefree and determined to rescue me...from you. Oh, it seemed such a good idea. I had it all worked out. We would marry and play at keeping house and play at being parents. I think I thought of having children rather as having a new set of dolls to play with.

'Things went badly wrong when we went to the inn. Well, you saw it! He started drinking brandy right away in great gulps. I had to...to go somewhere. I meant to tell him I had changed my mind. But when I returned, he had taken off all his clothes and was lying on the bed. It was terrible.

'I shook him and he staggered to his feet. I heard you knocking at the door. I was trying to help him pull on his Inexpressibles when you burst into the room. And then, as you know, he simply j-jumped th-through the *w-window.*'

Patricia began to laugh and laugh, the tears running down her face. 'It is not at all funny,' said Lord Charles, sitting down beside her. But, as she continued to laugh, it struck Lord Charles as being exquisitely funny as well, and added to that was exhilaration at the knowledge that the captain had left her untouched. He felt happiness going to his head like wine. They clung to each other, laughing helplessly, their faces lit red, blue, and gold as the fireworks burst in the sky far above their heads.

'Oh, how silly I am,' gasped Patricia finally. 'What will everyone think of us?'

'There is no one here to see us,' he said, his voice low and quiet.

Patricia gave a little shiver of apprehension and stood up quickly, her shawl falling from about her shoulders.

He picked it up and stood behind her and draped it gently over her shoulders, his hands coming to rest on her upper arms. They stood very still, each intensely aware of the other.

He unwound a white silk rose from her hair and put it into his waistcoat pocket. She turned and looked up into his face. He looked sad and withdrawn.

They walked in silence back to the box, each deep in thought.

'What is happening to me?' wondered Patricia desperately.

Lord Charles looked up as they approached the box. There was no sign of either of the governesses, the Lucases had gone, and the colonel had not returned. Lit up as if on a small stage sat Mrs Chalmers and

Mary. Both were staring straight ahead. Mrs Chalmers' face had a high flush and Mary's face was set in a mask of disapproval. They looked as if they had been quarrelling.

Lord Charles went quickly to Mary's side, explaining that the colonel had lost Patricia and that he had stayed to escort her. He apologized earnestly for his absence until Mary's stiff face began to relax.

'Where are Patricia's governesses?' asked Lord Charles, looking about.

'Miss Sinclair, that good and kind woman,' said Mrs Chalmers, 'felt it her duty to go to try to find you. As for Miss Simpkin! The most dreadful old roué called up to her and she went off with him, gasping and twittering she would not be long. She is a most unsuitable female and not at all like any governess *I* would employ.'

'But she is kind and has a good heart,' said Patricia.

'So *you* say,' said Mrs Chalmers rudely.

Miss Sinclair eventually reappeared with the colonel and the pair of them went into a long involved conversation about how they had tried to find Patricia, how they had called and searched, until Patricia not only began to feel very guilty but looked it. Mary studied Patricia's downcast face and her own grew stiff and hard again.

'I would like to leave,' she said.

'We will need to find Miss Simpkin first,' said Lord Charles. 'Which way did she go? And where are the Lucases?'

'Miss Simpkin went over in that direction,' said Mrs Chalmers, pointing toward the river. 'And a boy came with a message to say the Lucases were gone home.'

Lord Charles set off. He came on Miss Simpkin by chance. She was sitting on a bench in one of the smaller walks with an elderly gentleman by her side. Lord Charles recognized her companion as Sir Egbert Truebury, a rip whose son, Geoffrey, had recently been involved in some scandal over cheating at cards.

Despite the gloom of the walk, Lord Charles noticed the little governess's face had gone quite white under her rouge.

Sir Egbert lumbered to his feet as Lord Charles came striding up.

'Evening,' he wheezed. 'Just chatting to the little lady. Knew each other a long time ago, heh!'

'Are you ready to leave, Miss Simpkin?' asked Lord Charles.

'Yes, yes,' she said faintly.

'Don't forget what I told you,' said Sir Egbert, wagging a finger playfully at Miss Simpkin, who shrank back as if he waved a dagger at her.

Miss Simpkin got to her feet and trotted off with Lord Charles. 'Have you known Sir Egbert long?' he asked.

'Yes,' said Miss Simpkin breathlessly. 'Not that I have seen him for *years*.'

'You ran some sort of seminary before coming to Burnham House, did you not?'

'Yes,' squeaked Miss Simpkin.

'Was it not a profitable concern? I should think having one's own seminary infinitely preferable to earning your pay in someone else's house.'

'I found the strain of managing so many girls too much for me,' said Miss Simpkin. 'I sold up.'

He walked on, wondering why the sale had not been enough to set her up for life.

He was aware of her nervousness and uneasiness.

'If you are ever in any trouble,' he said, 'I would like you to know you can rely on me.'

'Thank you, my lord.' There was more

than a hint of tears in her voice and Lord Charles looked at her curiously. But she averted her face and scurried forward toward the box where the rest of Lord Charles's party sat waiting.

Lord Charles was very silent. This caused anguish in three bosoms. Patricia felt miserable and wished he would smile at her. Mary Chalmers thought her fiancé had behaved disgracefully and had no right to be so sullen. And Miss Sinclair thought Lord Charles was wishing his engagement at an end and blamed Patricia.

149

SIX

Patricia awoke late the following morning to find Miss Simpkin perched on the end of her bed. She struggled awake. 'Is anything the matter, Simpers?'

'No, my dear,' said the governess. 'It is just that we never seem to have a comfortable coze together like we did in the old days.'

'You pick the oddest times,' yawned Patricia. 'What do you wish to talk about?'

'Why, gentlemen,' said Miss Simpkin brightly. 'They are all enamoured of you, my love. You have taken London by storm.'

'The news of my fortune has no doubt taken London by storm as well,' said Patricia cynically. 'Do you know what I am doing today?'

'Mr Johnson said that Lord Charles is to take Miss Chalmers to the opera and that he has arranged that Colonel Sommers shall escort you.'

'Colonel Sommers is all very well in his

way,' said Patricia. 'He is handsome and kind and courteous, but so absent-minded! Half the time he does not seem to know where he is or whom he is with.' She stretched her arms lazily. 'Still, I had better look out something grand for the opera. There is that opera gown I started making. It only lacks some ribbon to trim it. Are you going out, Miss Simpkin? Perhaps you could buy some for me.'

'I was hoping we could perhaps go out together,' said Miss Simpkin. 'I long to have an ice at Gunter's. It would not take us very long and you have no arrangements for the afternoon.'

'Perhaps Lord Charles means to take me driving,' said Patricia hopefully.

'No, he is taking Miss Chalmers and her mother to the Park.'

Patricia turned away to hide her disappointment. 'In that case, Simpers, I shall take you to Gunter's and then you can help me choose ribbons for my gown.'

Gunter's, the famous confectioners in Berkeley Square, was crowded. It was about the only place in London where ladies could go to eat cakes and ices unescorted without occasioning comment.

'What is the time?' asked Miss Simpkin

as soon as they were seated.

'Two o'clock,' said Patricia, squinting at the fob watch pinned to her bosom. 'You keep looking this way and that. Are you expecting someone?'

'No,' said Miss Simpkin nervously. 'No, no. Why should I?'

'Silly old thing,' thought Patricia. Aloud, she said, 'Miss Sinclair was quite cross when I said I didn't want her to come with us. She is becoming a bit like a jailor. For some reason, she disapproves of me.'

'I never liked her, you know,' said Miss Simpkin. 'So rigid. All that learning. It addles the brain so.'

'But learning is your stock in trade,' said Patricia.

'But *genteel* subjects. Not geometry and Greek. Only gentlemen should learn *those*.'

Patricia ordered ices. After a time she said, 'Do eat yours. It is melting on your plate. Why do you keep looking about you?'

'I love seeing all the Fashionables. Of all marvellous things! Here is Mr Geoffrey Truebury.'

Patricia looked up and saw a foppish young man approaching. 'Must we meet him...?' she started to say, but Miss

Simpkin was already waving to the young man.

'Pon rep, Miss Simpkin,' said the young exquisite, swaggering up. 'You must present me to this fair charmer.'

'Certainly,' said Miss Simpkin eagerly. 'My love, I wish to present Mr Geoffrey Truebury; Mr Truebury, Miss Patterson.'

He made Patricia an excellent leg, and then to her annoyance drew out a chair and sat down next to her.

He was a small gentleman, highly painted. The backs of his hands were stained brown with walnut juice and the palms were dyed a delicate pink. He had very long, very pointed, polished nails. His portly figure was encased in a bright blue coat with an amazingly high collar. His shirt points were high enough to deserve the nickname 'patricides.'

He smelled strongly of musk and his teeth were bad. His hair was back-combed into a crest on the top of his head.

'I am the most fortunate of men,' he fluted. 'Dazzled by your beauty, Miss Patterson. Gad's 'Oonds, that I am. Nothing can compare to your beauty. Not the sun...er...the moon...trees, all that sort of thing,' he ended lamely.

'Unfortunately, you are arrived just as we are leaving,' said Patricia firmly. 'I am afraid Miss Simpkin does not relish Gunter's ices. She has not touched hers.'

'But I love it when it's melted,' said Miss Simpkin. 'Do wait until I am finished.'

'You haven't even started,' said Patricia, glaring.

Miss Simpkin picked up her spoon and began to eat little tiny drops of melted ice with maddening slowness.

'I believe I shall have the pleasure of seeing you at the opera tonight,' said Mr Truebury. 'And at Lady Blessington's on the morrow.'

'You are better informed than I,' said Patricia. '*Are* we going to Lady Blessington's, Miss Simpkin?'

Miss Simpkin choked slightly and mumbled, 'I believe so.'

'My dear Miss Patterson,' said Mr Truebury, 'pray allow me to be your cavalier and escort you to Lady Blessington's on the morrow. I should like it above all things. Consider myself honoured.'

'My guardian is escorting me, Mr Truebury, so I am in no need of an escort.'

Mr Truebury tried to take Patricia's

hand. She gave him a startled look and rose to her feet. 'Come along, Miss Simpkin,' she said firmly.

'But my ice,' protested Miss Simpkin. 'I have hardly begun to eat it.'

'Then you should not be so slow. Good day to you, Mr Truebury.'

Patricia marched to the door of the confectioner's. She turned around impatiently, waiting for Miss Simpkin to follow her.

But Miss Simpkin was leaning over Mr Truebury, muttering something. He replied sharply, his gaze malevolent.

Then the little governess rushed off to join Patricia.

'What was all that about?' demanded Patricia. 'What a truly repulsive young man.'

'Oh, no, you must not say that. He is of sterling worth. Quite the sweetest and prettiest of young men in town.'

'How was he so *au fait* with all my arrangements? Even I did not know about going to Lady Blessington's.'

Miss Simpkin hesitated, turned red, and then said in a rush, 'Well, don't you see, Lady Blessington must have told *him*. It is all very simple.'

'What I am about to tell you is also very simple. You are not to encourage that young man to speak to me again.'

To Patricia's horror, Miss Simpkin began to cry. 'I did not mean to offend,' she gulped. 'You do not understand. I was very fond of his father once.'

'You ninny,' sighed Patricia. 'I shall be civil to him when I see him, but do not arrange any more chance meetings.'

'I didn't—'

'Oh, yes you did. Dry your eyes or you will never be able to help me choose my ribbons!'

A fine drizzling rain had started to fall as Lord Charles entered the Park with Mary Chalmers beside him. It suited his dark mood, which even the absence of Mrs Chalmers could not lift.

'That is the trouble with these phaetons,' said his beloved, looking contemptuously from her high perch at one of the most dashing carriages in London. 'No protection from the elements.'

'Then it seems I must take you home again.'

'That would be much more pleasant,' she smiled. 'We can sit in front of the fire and have a comfortable coze with Mama.'

'My love, after we are married, you cannot expect to see your mother every day, and so perhaps it might be better if we found ways to be a little more on our own.'

'But of *course* I shall see Mama every day after we are married. She will be living with us.'

'She will *what?*'

'But I understood you *knew*,' said Mary. 'She is a widow and cannot be left on her own with only the servants for company.'

Lord Charles frowned but said nothing. It was not unusual for a man of his rank and position to find he was expected to house his wife's relatives as well as his own. The stately homes of England abounded with in-laws, poor relations, eccentric uncles, and half-crazed spinster aunts. Then he had to admit to himself that for some reason he had expected Mary to *want* to be alone with him. He had almost been on the point of asking her if she did not love him.

Which was ridiculous.

There had never been any question of love on either side. He had chosen a suitable lady of good birth and she had accepted him because he was of her class and accounted a catch. Sometimes, of course, people were lucky...like the Lucases. But usually one married to continue one's name, or to add to one's land or fortune.

He realized Mary had begun to talk about Patricia. 'She needs something serious to occupy her mind,' Mary was saying.

'Patricia has already studied a great deal,' said Lord Charles. 'She is immensely talented and can play the pianoforte and sing like an angel.'

'Sometimes we have talents of which we have long been unaware until one day we discover them,' said Mary.

He thought about Patricia's flirtatious remark. But Mary could hardly be talking about love.

'You have discovered such a one?'

Mary smiled modestly, a small, curved smile. 'I have recently discovered I have a small talent as a poet.'

They had just arrived outside Mary's home. Lord Charles felt he must escape. He did not want to sit and talk to Mrs Chalmers.

'If you will excuse me...' he began as he led Mary up to her door.

'You are surely not thinking of leaving before paying your respects to Mama!' exclaimed Mary. 'Besides, I want to read you my latest poem.'

'I shall not stay very long,' he sighed. 'I must confess to feeling a trifle unwell.'

'Mama will give you some of her rhubarb pills,' said Mary, leading the way inside.

Lord Charles looked about him. How odd that this home, which had always seemed to him before a haven of peace and quiet, should now seem so bleak.

'Here is Lord Charles come to see you, Mama,' said Mary, untying her bonnet and shaking the raindrops from it. 'I have told him of my secret work and he is avid to hear my latest composition.'

Mrs Chalmers looked at Lord Charles. He looked avid to escape.

'I do not think his lordship is in the mood to listen to poetry,' said Mrs Chalmers cautiously.

'Of course he is,' said Mary, going to a desk in the corner and taking out two sheets of paper. 'Now, this poem was inspired by Fashion. I fear you gentlemen think we ladies care for nothing but dress.

Miss Patterson, for example, shows too much interest in the fleeting vagaries of fashion. I have called my poem, "Drab Bonnets".'

'My dear, I think Lord Charles would like something to drink,' pleaded Mrs Chalmers.

'No, no. Poem first and drink afterward,' said Mary roguishly.

'This is awful! This is terrible!' thought Lord Charles. 'I must have been mad. I don't want to marry her.'

Mary delicately cleared her throat and began.

Drab Bonnets

They may cant of costumes, and of brilliant
headdresses,
À la Grecque—à la Françoise—or what else
they will;
They may talk of tiaras that glitter on
tresses
Enwreathed by the Graces, and braided with
skill;
Yet to my partial glance, I confess the drab
bonnet
Is the loveliest of any—and most when it
bears

160

Not only the gloss of neatness upon it—
But, beneath—the expression Benevolence
wears!
Then let Fashion exult in her vapid vagaries,
From her fascination my favourite is free;
Be folly's the headgear that momently varies,
But a Bonnet of drab is the sweetest to me.

Though stately the ostrich plume, gracefully
throwing
Its feathery flashes of light on the eye;
Though tasty and trim the straw bonnet when
glowing
With ribbons so glossy of various dye,
Yet still I must own though—

'Lord Charles, is anything the matter?'
He had his face completely covered by
his handkerchief.

He removed his handkerchief. His face
went through several strange contortions
before he rose to his feet and gasped, 'I
must leave. Terribly ill.'
Mary looked after him in surprise and
dismay as he fled the room.
Lord Charles found it very hard not to
burst out into hysterical laughter. It was
all so awful. His life stretched out in

front of him, a life of endless evenings listening to Mary reading her poetry while Mrs Chalmers complained about her rheumatism.

Miss Sinclair wandered slowly through Lord Charles's house in Cavendish Square indulging in one of her favourite dreams. She liked to imagine she was mistress of the house. Her hand slid over the silk of the upholstery, her eyes admired the statuary and paintings. She pushed open doors, inspecting the bedrooms. As if drawn by a magnet, her feet moved toward Lord Charles's bedroom. She gently pushed over the door and went inside. It was a very masculine room with a massive four-poster bed. The hangings were dark red. Fire-light glinted on a beaten brass fender and a Turkish carpet covered the floor.

And then the door opened and Lord Charles's Swiss valet, Edouard, walked in. He was a thin sallow man with clever black eyes. Miss Sinclair did not like him and distrusted him simply because he was a foreigner.

He stopped at the sight of Miss Sinclair. 'What are *you* doing here?' he demanded. His voice had only a very faint accent.

'I came to see that everything was in order,' said Miss Sinclair.

He picked up the evening waistcoat Lord Charles had worn to Vauxhall and started to brush it. 'You are too busy about the affairs of everyone else,' said Edouard, looking at the governess with contempt. 'Well, now that you've poked into everything, why don't you leave?'

'You forget yourself,' gasped Miss Sinclair.

'Not I. We are both upper servants, although some of us like to fancy ourselves as better than we are.' He poked his fingers into Lord Charles's waistcoat pockets and then drew out a crumpled white silk rose. He looked at it with a smile and teased out the petals.

'I'll take that,' said Miss Sinclair. 'That is one of the roses Miss Patterson was wearing in her hair last night.'

The valet gave her a long steady look and then carefully laid the rose on the table beside the bed

Miss Sinclair blushed to the roots of her hair. 'It does not mean anything,' she said. 'It is not a keepsake. Miss Patterson no doubt dropped it.'

'Then it is up to his lordship to return it to her,' said Edouard. 'That way neither of us will make any clumsy mistakes.'

He looked at Miss Sinclair with his clever black eyes, noticing her anger and distress, and turned away and began to arrange articles on the toilet table.

'Very suitable,' he murmured. 'Miss Patterson is an heiress and is young and beautiful.'

'You forget, Lord Charles is engaged.'

'For the moment—yes.'

Miss Sinclair hurriedly left the room. She could hardly wait for Patricia to return.

Patricia, still irritated with Miss Simpkin, viewed Miss Sinclair's flushed and angry face and wished herself rid of both governesses. She held up a hand as Miss Sinclair would have burst into speech.

'Give me time to remove my bonnet and draw breath before you start lecturing me. I know you are about to lecture me, for the tip of your nose is red.'

Miss Sinclair waited impatiently while Patricia removed her wet bonnet and spencer. 'Now,' said Patricia.

'I happened to be in Lord Charles's bedroom,' said Miss Sinclair, 'and his valet was brushing the waistcoat he wore last night. Before my eyes, he removed from the pocket one of the silk roses you were wearing in your hair.'

She waited hopefully for Patricia to say she must have dropped it, and she did not know how he came to have it. But Patricia stood very still, a tender smile on her lips. She was remembering the arbour in Vauxhall, and how he had taken the rose from her hair.

'Well?' demanded the governess furiously.

'He took it from my hair last night,' said Patricia dreamily.

'No, no,' gasped Miss Sinclair. 'He is engaged to Miss Chalmers. A gentleman like Lord Charles would not do such a thing.'

'You are quite right,' said Patricia, giving herself a little shake. 'I must have dropped it.'

'You are sure?'

Patricia's face hardened. 'Miss Sinclair, I am no longer a schoolroom miss. You are not to question me and cross-examine me, and, furthermore, your adoration of Lord Charles has become embarrassing.'

'*My* adoration? Do not be stupid,' said Miss Sinclair, suddenly hating Patricia.

'Just be careful you do not overstep the mark,' said Patricia. 'And do not preach propriety to me, Miss Sinclair, until you have fully learned it yourself.'

Miss Sinclair rushed from the room, slamming the door behind her. Patricia sat down. She found her legs were trembling.

She wondered what to do about Lord Charles, she wondered what to do about herself, and then she found she could not bear to think and worry anymore.

She looked out the opera gown and carried it with her new ribbons and workbasket down to the drawing room.

Lord Charles found her there when he returned some ten minutes later. He stood in the doorway watching her. She was stitching busily, sage green silk spilling over her lap. Ribbons and lace hung from her workbasket. There was a cheerful fire burning and a large vase of lilacs on a table perfumed the air. Fashion magazines lay piled on the table along with some of Patricia's well-worn Greek and Latin primers.

She looked up and saw him. Their eyes met. Patricia felt held and trapped in that steady green gaze. Her heart hammered and the palms of her hands grew damp.

And then he gave her a queer little jerky nod of his head and walked away.

'I will not be attracted by her,' Lord Charles told himself furiously. 'I must rediscover what it was that attracted me to Mary in the first place.'

But it was Mary's very absence of femininity which had attracted him so strongly. The neat order of her dress, her calm remarks, and her repose had all drawn a man who had had enough of frivolous girls.

But that evening he found his eyes had been opened to her faults and it seemed as if he would never be able to close them again. The opera was equal to Almack's Assembly Rooms in that the audience was hand-picked by a stern committee. People came to be seen and admired.

But Mary, thought Lord Charles wearily as they walked along Fop's Alley to their box, was neither interested in dress nor in the music. Through the whole performance of *Don Giovanni* she sat like a stone while Patricia leaned over the box, drinking in the music, her gown of heavy sage green silk ornamented with gold ribbons spread about her.

A supper and ball were to be held in the opera house after the performance. Persuading himself it was his duty to dance with his ward, Lord Charles forgot to ask Mary first. Mary sought out Miss Sinclair, who was sitting in the row of chaperones, and drew her aside.

'I am afraid my fiancé is making a spectacle of himself with Miss Patterson,' said Mary. 'It is very bad manners not to lead me into the opening set.'

'I quite agree,' said Miss Sinclair earnestly. 'One would think Lord Charles would be wary of her after the scandal that sent us both to America.'

'What scandal?' asked Mary eagerly.

Miss Sinclair bit her lip. The temptation to tell Miss Chalmers about the soldier was very great. But Lord Charles had sworn her to secrecy.

'I cannot tell you,' she said. 'But Patricia's real character is coming to the surface. Lord Charles's valet showed me a white silk rose he had just taken from his lordship's waistcoat pocket. I recognized it as being one of the flowers Patricia wore in her hair in Vauxhall. I taxed Patricia with it and she finally admitted she had merely dropped it and he picked it up, but in *such* a pert and rude way that I fear she was lying.'

Mary found herself becoming very angry

168

indeed. Lord Charles could not break off the engagement—no gentleman would dream of doing such a thing—but he had been cross and out of sorts of late, and it was all Patricia's fault.

'Is Miss Patterson enamoured of Lord Charles?' asked Mary abruptly.

'I do not know. She has never confided her thoughts to me. The only person she has ever really confided in as far as I know is Miss Margaret Munroe of Boston. Patricia writes her very long letters.'

'I would dearly love to read one of those letters,' said Mary thoughtfully. 'After all, there would be no harm in glancing through the contents, Miss Sinclair. If Miss Patterson is pure of heart, then there will be nothing in her letters to shock anyone. Not that I could...er...*ask* you to do such a thing. A lady such as yourself must surely shrink from such a distasteful task.'

'Lord Charles said he hoped he could depend on my loyalty to you,' said Miss Sinclair. 'As her governess, I feel I am entitled to read her post.'

'Thank you. You will not find me ungrateful.' Mary pressed Miss Sinclair's hand warmly. 'In fact, after our marriage, I might engage a companion. Gentlemen are away at their clubs and politics so often. Mama will reside with us, but it would be pleasant to have a female companion of my own age.'

She pressed Miss Sinclair's hand more warmly and smiled into her eyes.

'I will do anything you wish,' said Miss Sinclair tremulously.

On the road home from the opera house, Miss Sinclair and Mary joined forces to try to make Patricia appear as silly as possible. With an edge to her voice, Miss Sinclair teased Patricia about her absorption with clothes. Mary Chalmers said Nobility of Spirit was above Fashion and discoursed at length on the subject, until Patricia said sweetly, 'I am sure a gown of this sage green colour would suit *you*, Miss Chalmers. It would match the colour of your eyes.'

'My eyes are grey,' snapped Mary.

'Behave yourself,' snapped Miss Sinclair.

'All of you, behave yourselves,' said Lord Charles. 'I am too tired to listen to your whining and bickering.'

Silence fell on the occupants of the carriage. Lord Charles refused Mrs Chalmers' invitation to enter her home and take tea, and left Mary and her mother on their doorstep with only the briefest of farewells.

When they arrived at Lord Charles's home in Cavendish Square, Patricia turned to Miss Sinclair and said, 'Please leave me alone with my guardian. There is something I wish to say to him in private.'

Miss Sinclair bridled. 'I do not think that wise, Patricia. It is not at all the thing that a girl of your age should be alone with a gentleman, unchaperoned.'

'Leave us,' said Lord Charles curtly, 'before you manage to offend me as well as Miss Patterson by your behaviour.'

'I am sure, my lord, that I—'

'For pity's sake...*go*.'

Miss Sinclair gave a choked sob and fled.

'Now, Patricia,' said Lord Charles, leading the way into the drawing room, 'what do you want to speak to me about?'

'We are to go to a Lady Blessington's tomorrow, I believe.'

'Yes.'

'And just how many hundreds of people are going with us?'

'Let me see—I have arranged for you to

be escorted by Colonel Brian Sommers—'

'You might have asked me...'

'And I shall take Miss Chalmers—'

'*And* Mrs Chalmers. Do you wish me to marry Colonel Sommers?'

Lord Charles frowned. 'He is highly suitable, but it is up to you to decide.'

'He might forget to turn up for his own wedding.'

'Did you want to see me alone to criticize the poor colonel?'

'No. I do not want Miss Sinclair to go with me.'

Lord Charles looked at Patricia thoughtfully. 'As you will,' he said at last. 'Colonel Sommers will be driving an open carriage, so you will not need a chaperone. Lady Blessington's is in Kensington. If, however, it should chance to rain, then you will need to have some lady with you in the carriage.'

'Will you please tell Miss Sinclair she is not to go?'

'I shall leave that task to the excellent Mr Johnson.'

The next day, as yet unaware she was to be left behind, Miss Sinclair pulled on her gloves and bonnet, preparatory to

172

making her way downstairs. The affair at Lady Blessington's was to be a breakfast, and breakfasts were always held at three in the afternoon, despite their name, and often went on until the small hours of the morning.

It was a beautiful day, warm and sunny. Miss Sinclair thought about reading Patricia's correspondence. But what had seemed a just thing to do the night before, now seemed mean and shabby.

There was a scratching at the door. She called, 'Come in.'

Mr Johnson entered, straightening his cravat.

'Am I late, Mr Johnson?' asked Miss Sinclair. 'Is everyone waiting for me?'

'I am afraid not,' said Mr Johnson awkwardly. 'My lord sends his compliments and begs to inform you that your presence will not be needed today.'

'What is this? Is that Simpkin woman to go in my stead?'

'No, Miss Sinclair. Colonel Brian Sommers is to escort Miss Patterson, and seeing that they will be travelling to Kensington in an open carriage, it was felt Miss Patterson could dispense with the services of a chaperone.'

'Nonsense!' said Miss Sinclair briskly. 'I shall speak to Miss Patterson. You will find she does not wish me to stay behind.'

Mr Johnson sighed. 'I fear it was Miss Patterson's particular request that you did not attend the breakfast.'

'Oh!' Miss Sinclair sat down abruptly, her face flaming.

Mr Johnson smoothed his hair with a nervous hand. 'I have some free time this afternoon, Miss Sinclair, and would be very honoured if you would care to walk with me in the Park.'

But Miss Sinclair did not appear to hear him. She sat with her fists clenched. 'The ingratitude,' she muttered. 'The sheer ingratitude.'

Mr Johnson looked at her sadly and then quietly left the room.

Patricia was very annoyed with her guardian. He had already left half an hour before, telling her blithely that no doubt the colonel would be along any minute. But so far there had been no sign of him.

She was just debating whether to hire a hack and pursue Lord Charles to Kensington when Colonel Sommers rolled up in front of the house driving a swan-neck phaeton. Patricia ran out to meet him.

'You are late,' she said.

'Am I?' exclaimed the colonel from his high perch. 'Dear me.' He took out his watch and squinted at it and then shook it. 'Never did work,' he said cheerfully.

'Well, now that you *are* here,' said Patricia, 'may we go?'

'Yes certainly. Do you mind if my tiger assists you up? I dare not leave the reins. Cattle very fresh, y'know.'

'Anything,' said Patricia, glaring up at him, 'so long as we *leave.*'

'Assist the lady,' called the colonel over his shoulder. A wizened and diminutive cockney jumped down from the backstrap and went around to where Patricia stood.

'Bleedin' 'diculous,' he muttered under his breath. 'This rig'll get us no further'n 'Yde Park toll.'

'*What* did you say?' demanded Patricia icily, not being at all used to the free and easy speech of certain London Tigers.

'Nuffink,' he said, helping her up.

Patricia hung on tightly to the side of the carriage as they set off. She hoped she would not be travel sick. The carriage was so very high and so very well sprung that it swung from side to side like a ship on a stormy sea.

'Designed it myself,' yelled the colonel above the noise of the wheels.

'An' a raht mess you made o' it, too,' Patricia thought she heard the tiger mutter from behind.

But the vehicle seemed designed for speed, and, once they were through Hyde Park toll, the colonel said he was going to 'spring 'em.'

There was a moan from the tiger as they shot off along the road.

The carriage lurched and swayed dangerously. 'Slow your pace, sir,' cried Patricia.

'What?' asked the colonel, taking his gaze from the road ahead.

'Don't speak to 'im, missus,' screamed the tiger. 'Don't take 'is mind off wot he's doin'.'

'I said, slow your pace,' shouted Patricia.

'Yes, it is a fine day,' beamed the colonel. 'By George, Miss Patterson, that's the most fetching bonnet I ever saw.'

'My Gawd, look out!' shouted the tiger.

Patricia screamed. They were heading straight for an oncoming cart, laden with hay.

The colonel saw the expression of horror on Patricia's face. Too late, he turned his attention back to the road. His horses reared and swerved. The side of the phaeton struck the side of the heavy farm cart. Patricia was thrown sideways from her high perch on top of the hay. As the colonel's carriage shattered like matchwood, he was dragged down onto the road, still holding onto the reins. The tiger had somersaulted backward and was sitting in the dusty road, cursing and shaking his fists.

Patricia lay on top of the hay, digging her fingers into it so that she would not slide off. She felt as if all the breath had been knocked from her body.

At last, she raised her head. Colonel Sommers was being helped to his feet. Blood was streaming from a cut on his forehead and his clothes were dusty and torn. The shattered carriage lay in pieces in the road. The horses, miraculously unhurt, had been led to the side.

He looked about in a dazed way. 'I am here!' shouted Patricia.

The driver of the farm cart came around the side and glared up at her. 'What are you doin' up on my cart? I've enough on me plate without fancy morts fooling about. Some gentry cove near sent me to my Maker.' Patricia struggled up to her knees. 'You are fortunately unhurt,' she said, 'and so is your cart.'

She turned her attention back to the colonel. 'Pore young man,' a motherly woman was saying. 'Best walk him back along to St George's Hospital.' This suggestion was cheerfully taken up by the sympathetic crowd.

'What about me?' she shouted as the colonel was helped off down the road.

'I dunno, miss,' said the tiger, grinning up at her. He had come to the side of the cart. 'I told 'is nibs that there carriage was a death trap. But would 'e listen to me? Naw! Designed it 'isself and as proud o' it as if 'e'd given birth to it. I needs to stay with the 'orses.'

'Help me down,' said Patricia.

'You'd best slide,' said the tiger, 'an' I'll ketch you.'

Patricia slid down the hay into the arms of the tiger.

'Miss Patterson,' called a languid voice, 'may I be of assistance?'

Patricia turned around eagerly and then her face fell as she saw Mr Geoffrey

Truebury leaning out of a carriage.

'There was an accident,' said Patricia.

'I am going to Lady Blessington's. May I escort you?'

Patricia looked doubtfully at Mr Truebury's closed carriage, but the desire to catch up with Lord Charles, to see him again as soon as possible, was very strong.

'Thank you,' she said. Mr Truebury's footman jumped down and opened the door and Patricia climbed in.

At first, she was too busy picking straws out of her gown, straightening her crushed bonnet, and tucking wisps of hair under it, to answer Mr Truebury's questions. But at last she gave him a brief account of the accident.

'Monstrous!' said Mr Truebury. '*I* would have treated an angel like yourself like glass. I cannot understand Lord Charles—leaving you in the hands of such an irresponsible escort.'

That had been exactly what Patricia had been thinking, but she found she disliked Mr Truebury even more than she had done in Gunter's, and leaped to the colonel's defence.

'It was all my fault,' she said, 'I distracted Colonel Sommers by talking to him. He did not have his eyes on the road.'

'Ah, that is understandable,' said Mr Truebury, seizing hold of Patricia's hand. 'Demme, if it ain't.'

Patricia snatched her hand away. 'I should not be in a closed carriage with you, Mr Truebury,' she said stiffly, 'and so I must beg you to behave with decorum.'

'It is hard for me to do so,' cried Mr Truebury passionately, 'when I am faced with the many charms of the lady I hope to make my wife.'

'Mr *Truebury!*'

'Furthermore, I know you are not indifferent to me,' he went on.

'I am grateful to you, Mr Truebury, for escorting me to Kensington, but I shall not accept any man of whom my guardian has not approved. I suggest you approach him before speaking of the subject again.'

'Miss Simpkin would have me believe you were too modern a miss to stand much on ceremony.'

'I shall speak very strongly to Miss Simpkin when I return. She had no right to discuss me with you or anybody else. How do you come to be on such familiar terms with my governess?'

'A gentleman such as myself is not in

the habit of being on familiar terms with any servant,' he said. 'Miss Simpkin was an...er...acquaintance of my father at one time.'

'Oh,' said Patricia, suddenly not wanting to know any more. 'Tell me all about yourself,' she added brightly, hoping that this might keep Mr Truebury fully occupied.

Mr Truebury was only too eager to oblige. He bragged of his success with the ladies with many sighs and rolling of his eyes. He claimed to be intimate with the Prince Regent and to have snubbed the great Brummell. He waxed more enthusiastic about his fame, his many talents, and his physical attributes, until he almost forgot Patricia was there. After all, he held such conversations with his reflection almost every day.

To Patricia, the journey to Lady Blessington's seemed to take forever, and to Mr Truebury to be over in a flash.

He made a great show of helping her down from the carriage, and was quite upset and disappointed when Lord Charles Gaunt who was standing with the other guests on the front lawn snatched her rudely away without sparing the gallant Mr Truebury so much as a glance.

'What are you about?' demanded Lord Charles furiously. 'Is this one of your hoydenish tricks? Where is Colonel Sommers?'

He marched her around the back of the house. He opened the french windows to a music room as he was talking and thrust her inside.

'If you would *listen!*' shouted Patricia. And she continued to shout at the top of her voice, a jumble of explanations about accidents and poor Colonel Sommers, his cheeky tiger, the impossible Mr Truebury, how he wanted to marry her—'As if I ever would!' ended Patricia, out of breath.

'Gently, quietly,' he said, beginning to laugh. 'Sit down, Patricia, and tell me the whole business from the beginning.'

Patricia sighed and sat down. He sat down next to her on a backless sofa and took her hand in his own. Somehow, she never even thought of snatching her hand away.

So she told her story over again, but this time she ended up demanding to know why Lord Charles thought Colonel Sommers such a fine chaperone since he was absent-minded, hard of hearing, and short-sighted.

'He is a man of sterling character and a

very loyal friend,' said Lord Charles, but at the same time he began to wonder whether he had invited the colonel to escort Patricia simply because he *knew* Patricia would not fall in love with him.

To change the subject, he added, 'I was distressed to see you arriving with such a fellow as Geoffrey Truebury. I trust he did not make a nuisance of himself.'

'He would have, had I not encouraged him to talk about himself.' Patricia hesitated. She had been about to say that Miss Simpkin appeared to have encouraged Mr Truebury, but she changed her mind for fear of getting the governess into trouble.

'What I tried to tell you,' she said, 'was that Mr Truebury proposed to me.'

'The devil he did!'

'I told him he must ask your permission first.'

'Quite right. I shall have a word with that young whipper-snapper. *And* Miss Simpkin, when we return home.'

'Miss Simpkin?' said Patricia taking her hand from his.

'Yes. She knows the family—or rather that awful old rip of a father. I found them together at Vauxhall.'

'I do not think Mr Truebury needs any encouragement from *anyone*,' said Patricia. 'He is quite capable of being pushing and obnoxious all on his own.'

'In other words, Miss Simpkin had nothing to do with it?'

'She would never do anything to harm me.'

Patricia stood up and crossed to a looking glass over the fireplace, and removed her bonnet. 'What a mess I am in!' she exclaimed. 'But I could have been killed, so a little death to my vanity is as nothing by comparison.'

He stood up, watching her as she teased her hair back into a fashionable style.

He slowly walked up and stood behind her. Patricia lowered her comb and looked at both their faces reflected in the glass. He put his hands on her shoulders and said, 'Patricia.'

She coloured and her breath began to come quick and fast.

'Patricia,' he said again, this time in a wondering voice.

He turned her about to face him. The room was quiet and still. A harpsichord stood gleaming in one corner, a shrouded harp in the other. Outside in the garden at the back of the house, away from the guests, a thrush swung on a branch heavy with lilac flowers, sending out a repetitive cascade of notes.

She looked up into his green eyes, suddenly wanting to tell him how sorry she was for the years of hate and how she had planned her revenge. But he took her face gently between his hands and bent his mouth to hers and she forgot about everything else. She felt as if she were turning slowly around as his kiss caused wave after wave of sensation to course through her body. He dropped his hands from her face and wrapped his arms tightly about her, holding her closely against him, feeling the throbbing and trembling of her body. He gave a little sigh and kissed her more deeply and with such an intensity of passion that when he finally raised his mouth, she clung to him like a drowning woman, gazing up at him with eyes blinded by emotion.

He sank to one knee in front of her and raised the hem of her dress to his lips. 'No!' cried Patricia. 'Do not kneel in front of me.'

He looked up and saw that her eyes were bright with tears. Patricia was thinking wretchedly of how she had dreamed of this moment, of how she would laugh at him and spurn him, but now all she wanted was to be held by him and kissed by him once more.

'You are right,' he said softly, rising to his feet and tilting her chin up. 'We should not be doing this. Oh, Patricia, I am engaged to Mary Chalmers and cannot get free unless she will release me. But if she will, marry me, Patricia, for no other woman will do. I have never loved anyone else before and am not likely to love anyone else in the future as much as I love you.'

Patricia clung to him, realizing with a desperate gladness that she loved him. Surely Mary would not want to go ahead and marry a man who did not love her.

There was the sound of approaching footsteps and they jumped apart. Patricia opened her mouth to tell him that she loved him, but the door opened and Lady Blessington walked in.

'I have been looking everywhere for you, Lord Charles,' she said. 'Miss Chalmers has been wondering what had become of you.'

Lady Blessington was a soft, fat woman

dressed in white muslin. She looked like a pillow tied in the middle. Her eyes swivelled to Patricia. 'And who is this?' she demanded.

'My ward, Miss Patterson,' said Lord Charles.

'*Indeed!*' Lady Blessington's small eyes swung from one face to the other, from Patricia's flushed and radiant one to Lord Charles's carefully guarded mask.

'Miss Patterson had an unfortunate accident on the way here. Colonel Sommers was hurt and so he will not be joining us.'

'We heard *all about* the accident,' said Lady Blessington, 'from dear Mr Truebury.'

All in that moment Patricia decided she did not like Lady Blessington. Anyone who referred to Mr Truebury as 'dear' could not be a very pleasant person.

'Ah, yes, that reminds me. Truebury,' said Lord Charles. 'I want a word with that young man.'

'Then come along,' said Lady Blessington. 'We are about to serve breakfast.'

They followed her through the house and out onto the front lawn, where people were already seated at long tables. Lord Charles went immediately to join Mary. Patricia was left to sit between two gentlemen she did not know. But the fact that Lord Charles had said he loved her spread like a warm glow throughout her body. The world had become a beautiful and exciting place. Soon this day would be over and she and Lord Charles would be able to leave Mary and her mother at their home and then go to Cavendish Square together.

Then, as she glanced idly about, she saw with surprise Mrs Grant with her daughters, Emily and Agnes. Emily smiled and waved, but Patricia, although she smiled back, experienced a little pang of dread. Emily and Agnes must know all about the gossip about herself and the captain. If they talked, then society would look at her with different eyes, and if she married Lord Charles they would all say it was because she had to.

Then the gentleman on her left turned and introduced himself. He was a fair and foolish young man, but extremely good-natured, and soon Patricia forgot her fears and began to enjoy herself.

After the breakfast was over, Patricia agreed to promenade with her new companion, a Mr Naith, through the grounds. At one point, she saw Lord

Charles take Mr Truebury aside. She could not hear what they were saying, but Mr Truebury's face became mottled with rage.

Later, she looked across to where Lord Charles was now standing with Mary. He smiled at her, and she smiled back, her whole face becoming alight with love. Startled, Mary looked from one to the other.

Patricia quickly turned her head away, furious with herself for having betrayed her emotions so openly. Then the Misses Grant came up to her and began to ply her with questions about America. Agnes was engaged to a squire who lived near Barminster and Emily to another local worthy, and they had merely come to town for two weeks to order their wedding clothes. They did not mention the scandal, and Patricia began to relax and enjoy their company.

SEVEN

Left to her own devices for the afternoon, Miss Sinclair decided to see if she could find anything Patricia had written to Margaret Munroe, but there was nothing at all in Patricia's bedroom—no half-finished letter and no diary of any description.

Feeling frustrated, she began to wish she had agreed to go for that walk with Mr Johnson and went in search of him. He was sorting through the late post and Miss Sinclair immediately saw one letter from America addressed to Patricia.

All thoughts of going for a walk fled. 'I see you have a letter for Miss Patterson, Mr Johnson,' said Miss Sinclair. 'I shall take it up to her room and leave it on her desk.'

'Thank you,' he said with a charming smile. 'I shall be going out shortly. Is there no hope that you might change your mind and accompany me?'

Miss Sinclair hesitated. She looked at him as if seeing him for the first time.

He was a pleasant and intelligent man. But then all her fury at Patricia came back into her mind and she said firmly, 'Perhaps another time, Mr Johnson. There are certain things this afternoon I must do.'

'Then I must wait and hope for another time,' he said.

Miss Sinclair picked up the letter and retreated with it upstairs to her own room.

She heated a paper knife at the fire and then gently opened the seal. The letter was from Margaret Munroe.

'Dear Patricia,' she read. 'I trust you are safely arrived and all goes well with you. Our poor little Boston must seem very Drab set against the Pleasures of London. Are you proceeding with your Great Revenge? If anyone can bring your wicked guardian to his knees, it is you, Patricia. Has he knelt in front of you yet and told you he loves you—and have you spurned him? I remember all the plots and plans we discussed to bring about the ruin of the wicked Lord Charles.

'I must confess, dear Patricia, I am worried that such a kind and pleasant lady such as yourself should be consumed with Hate. I hope our little plots and plans

191

were merely silly Girlish Schemes and that you have done nothing to bring them to Fruition. The Sermon in Church Sunday last was about the Folly of Revenge and the Suffering it can bring on the Vengeful, and I confess I felt alarmed on your behalf. Perhaps you will not even be in London yet when this letter arrives, although I am sending it on the very next ship.

'You are much missed by all of us here. Now to the gossip of the town. Tis said that Mr Devereux...'

Miss Sinclair slowly put down the letter. How dare that wicked Patricia try to ruin Lord Charles's life! Her duty lay plain before her. She would go to the Chalmers' house and await their return.

Had not Miss Sinclair been quite so zealous, she might have perhaps missed Mary's return. For the breakfast was not expected to be finished until early morning. But by eight in the evening, Mary, increasingly worried about the *atmosphere* between Lord Charles and Patricia, declared she had the headache and wanted to leave. An orchestra had arrived and there was to be dancing indoors in the ballroom, and Mary did not want to watch Lord Charles dancing with Patricia.

It was a silent party that travelled back to town. Lord Charles was desperately wondering how to extricate himself from his engagement, Patricia was longing to be alone with him again, Mrs Chalmers was silently blaming her daughter for being such a cold fish, and Mary could not remember being so angry since she was six years old and a visiting child took her doll away from her.

Mrs Chalmers pressed Lord Charles to 'step indoors' when they arrived, pointedly ignoring Patricia. But Lord Charles felt he could not bring matters to a head at that moment and he knew he would be honour-bound to do so if he sent Patricia home on her own and joined Mary and her mother.

He reminded Mary of her 'terrible headache' and said he would call on her the next morning since he had something important to discuss with her.

Mrs Chalmers noticed how Patricia's face lit up as he said this, and her heart sank.

When Patricia entered the house in Cavendish square, Lord Charles said gently, 'I do not trust myself to be alone with you, my love, until I have settled matters with Mary. Leave me before I forget I am an engaged man.'

Patricia smiled at him tremulously and then went lightly up the stairs to her room, elated and happy.

Lord Charles had just settled down in front of the fire in the library to read the correspondence when his butler came in to say that a footman had arrived from Miss Chalmers with an urgent message demanding his lordship's immediate presence.

He put down his letters and sighed wearily. Well, if he had to face her, perhaps it would be better to resolve things as soon as possible.

When he arrived at the Chalmers' house and was ushered into the drawing room, he raised his eyebrows in surprise to find Miss Sinclair sitting with Mary and her mother.

'I am glad you are come,' said Mary at her most stately. 'Miss Sinclair, this good and kind creature, has seen fit to open and read this letter.'

She held it out to him. 'Dear Patricia,' read Lord Charles. 'This is disgraceful!' he exclaimed. 'You have overstepped yourself, Miss Sinclair!'

'You must read on,' said Mary calmly,

'and you will find out why it was important to open it.'

Lord Charles read quickly through the first few paragraphs. Then he sat down and read slowly through them again.

He felt a black weight of grief and loss growing inside him. He had long been sure that the only interest he held for pretty young debutantes was his title and fortune. Patricia was a wealthy heiress and could marry a duke if she pleased. He had been so sure she really loved him. He should have known better.

Miss Sinclair shrank back in her chair as he raised his eyes. They were like emerald chips. 'I still say you had no right to open this letter, Miss Sinclair,' he said. 'Eavesdroppers, it is said, never hear any good of themselves, and Paul Prys cause pain and damage.

'You will go to Cavendish Square and tell Mr Johnson you are dismissed. I am not a vindictive man, so the pension I promised you will still be paid to you. Nor am I going to turn you out into the street until you have found somewhere to stay. If you have no relatives to go to, then ask Mr Johnson to find you lodgings as soon as possible.'

Miss Sinclair began to cry, hiccupping and sobbing that she had only been doing her duty.

'Lord Charles, how can you be so harsh?' cried Mary. 'Miss Sinclair may stay with me.' She put an arm about the sobbing governess. 'Come—I will show you to your room and Lord Charles may send your baggage.'

There was a heavy silence after they had left the room. Mrs Chalmers opened her mouth several times to say something, but Lord Charles was studying the letter again, his face grim and set.

After what seemed an age, Mary came in again looking flushed and triumphant.

'Poor Miss Sinclair is quite overset,' she said. 'I made her a hot posset and got her to lie down.'

'Leave us,' said Lord Charles quietly to Mrs Chalmers. She hesitated, looking at her daughter. Lord Charles got to his feet and went and silently held open the door.

Mrs Chalmers scurried past him, her head bowed.

'Now, Mary,' said Lord Chalmers, 'I feel you encouraged that silly woman in her folly.'

'And rightly,' said Mary calmly, 'as it turns out. You were about to make a cake of yourself over your ward.'

'Mary,' he said, 'have you never thought I might stray from you through the longing to hold a woman in my arms?'

The triumphant look left Mary's face and she took a step back from him. 'There will be plenty of time for *that* after we are married,' she said.

He felt cold rage burning inside him. Mary would not even pretend to care for him, and Patricia had made a fool of him.

'Then you had better get used to me,' he said grimly.

He caught her to him and forced his mouth down on hers. When he finally released her cold lips, she was trembling and shaken and staring at him as if he had just raped her.

Lord Charles gave a harsh laugh at the mixture of disgust and fright on her face. 'That was only a beginning,' he said. 'Only think, dear Mary, of the pleasures of the marriage bed.'

'You have spoiled everything,' said Mary after she had scrubbed her mouth with her handkerchief. 'I thought we would go on as we were—you and I and Mama. We were so comfortable before that Patricia creature arrived.'

'And I thought Mrs Chalmers was always present because *you* asked her to be there! Tell me, Mary, did you expect to remain a virgin even *after* our marriage?'

She simply stood looking at him, her face working.

'And to think I was worried about *your* feelings,' he said with deep disgust. 'Madam, will you send the notice of the termination of our engagement to the newspapers, or will I?'

'I will,' said Mary. 'You are a *beast.*'

Lord Charles left without looking back. He was in a murderous mood and was afraid that if he returned home immediately he would do something to Miss Patricia Patterson that he would regret for the rest of his life. He took himself off to his club to clear his head. But he started to drink to calm himself down and the more he drank, the more bitter and furious he became.

Patricia had been unable to sleep for excitement. She longed to share her happiness with someone but felt she had no right to until matters with

198

Mary were resolved. She kept running to her bedroom window every time she heard carriage wheels, hoping to see Lord Charles return, only to sit down again, disappointed.

At last she prepared for bed, and, sitting down at the dressing table, began to brush out her hair, remembering how odd and short it had been when she had first tried to wear it *à la Brutus*.

She heard the rumble of wheels on the cobbles below and ran to the window again.

Lord Charles was springing down from the box of his carriage, his face set and grim.

He strode into the house and a moment later Patricia heard him mounting the stairs.

She sat down again, her heart beating hard, longing to run to him.

Then she looked up in alarm as the door of her bedroom swung open.

Lord Charles leaned against the door jamb, looking at her, his green eyes blazing. His black hair was ruffled as if he had run his hands through it.

'Well, you slut,' he said. 'What have you to say to *this?*'

He threw Margaret Munroe's crumpled letter on the bed. Patricia picked it up. 'This is addressed to *me!*' she said furiously. 'Why did you open it?'

'*I* did not open it. But it is as well it was opened. Read it!'

Patricia read the opening paragraphs in dismay. A guilty blush rose to her cheeks.

'Aye, well you may blush,' he said savagely. 'I thought you innocent. You! A trollop who at the tender age of sixteen shares a bed in a sleazy inn with a redcoat. But what a fine actress you are. You fooled me with your act of dewy innocence.' He tore off his jacket as he spoke and threw it in a corner.

'What on earth do you think you are doing?' demanded Patricia.

'I am going to have a share of what you so freely gave to the British army.'

Patricia ran for the door.

He seized her arm and twisted it behind her back and looked down into her flushed and frightened face. Then he picked her up bodily and threw her on the bed.

She scrambled to the far side, but he jumped into the bed after her, caught her wriggling body, and jerked her into his arms. He rolled over until he was lying on top of her.

Patricia opened her mouth to scream, but he covered it with his own. Still kissing her savagely, he moved his body to her side and ripped her nightgown open from throat to hem. He then rolled on top of her again, the leather of his breeches cold against her thighs and his waistcoat buttons digging into her flesh. Panting and wriggling, Patricia fought her hardest to get free. Part of her frightened mind wondered whether she was really the trollop he thought her. For though he smelled abominably of brandy, though he was out to rape her, her treacherous body was beginning to respond to him despite her will.

He sensed her response and felt the shiver that ran through her body when his hand touched her breast and his kisses became more gentle and more searching.

'Not like this,' he whispered, raising his head at last. 'I am going to remove these clothes. You will not run away?'

Patricia shook her head dumbly, her eyes glinting with tears.

He quickly took off the rest of his clothes and then pressed her close against his naked body. He gently kissed her eyes and her nose and then her mouth again.

His mouth moved lower to her breast, and Patricia, overcome with a mixture of shame and passion and love, put her arms around him and said, 'Oh, Charles, don't be angry with me. I do love you so.'

He went very still.

Then he raised himself on one elbow and looked down at her, seeing her bruised mouth and the torn wreck of her muslin nightgown spread out on either side of her on the bed.

'Dear God,' he said, shaking his head. 'Oh, dear God.' He swung his legs out of bed and quickly pulled on his breeches.

'Charles!' whispered Patricia, but he walked straight out of the room.

Patricia cried for a long time. Then she rose and bathed her face and put on a clean nightgown. Picking up his shirt from the floor, she carried it to bed with her, and, cradling her cheek against it, cried herself to sleep.

Lord Charles Gaunt arose early, suffering from an abominable headache and a heavy conscience. He bitterly regretted his conduct. He had forgotten Patricia's youth. He thought ruefully that her pride must have been as savagely hurt when he arrived at Burnham House as his had hurt the evening before. He was sure she had said she loved him simply as a way to get through his madness, to bring him to his senses. Now he would have to marry her. If the servants had not known what was going on in Miss Patricia's bedroom then it would be a miracle. And even the most faithful of servants would talk.

He summoned Mr Johnson and told him to go and see Miss Sinclair and to find out whether she meant to remain with the Chalmers or whether she wished lodgings. He curtly outlined the reason for Miss Sinclair's dismissal.

From the cold look on Mr Johnson's face, Lord Charles knew his secretary thought the punishment too severe and that only his rigid notions of etiquette were preventing him from saying so.

Lord Charles decided to go and talk to the Lucases. He felt he could not bear to see Patricia, just yet.

Worn out with crying and emotion, Patricia slept until nine. She was awakened by Miss Simpkin. The little governess was looking more cheerful than she had done since the evening at Vauxhall.

She chattered on about how Mr Johnson was ordering the servants to pack Miss Sinclair's trunks. 'She has been dismissed. I wonder why?'

Patricia realized that Miss Sinclair must have been the one who opened the letter and read it.

She pretended to listen to Miss Simpkin's chatter, but her head felt strange and heavy. She, Patricia, had given Lord Charles a disgust of her from which he would never recover. She had taken that splendid present of love and thrown it away.

'Miss Simpkin,' she said at last, 'I am feeling unwell. Please leave me.'

Miss Simpkin began to fuss. Could she bring dear Patricia a hot posset? Might she bathe her temples with cologne?

Patricia shook her head wearily. She went to her writing desk and opened the drawer and took out several guineas.

'Please go and buy yourself something pretty, Simpers,' she said.

'But I *couldn't*,' bleated Miss Simpkin.

'Oh, yes you could,' said Patricia, giving her a gentle shove in the direction of the door. 'Go to Gunter's and eat *all* the melted ices you wish.'

After many more thanks and protests, Miss Simpkin left. She felt she *deserved* something. After all, she had come to terms with her conscience. The Trueburys could threaten her as much as they liked, but she would not do as they asked.

Patricia sat down wearily and stared at the room through the prism of her tears. She heard the street door slam and ran to the window, dashing the tears from her eyes.

Lord Charles was striding away across the square. If ever a man's back looked angry, it was his, thought Patricia wretchedly.

All at once she longed to escape and began to wonder how she might achieve it. She received a generous allowance from Lord Charles, since her money did not become her own until her twenty-first birthday, but it was not enough to keep her at some inn or hotel for very long, since Lord Charles would stop paying her allowance into the bank as soon as he discovered her missing.

But the desire to escape was very great. Patricia decided to go downstairs and find Mr Johnson and ask how long Lord

Charles was expected to be away.

But as she entered the hall, the butler was just opening the door to Mr Truebury, who pushed his way past as soon as he saw Patricia. He had seen Lord Charles leave and had come for one last desperate attempt to ingratiate himself with the heiress.

Patricia was about to order the butler to show Mr Truebury the outside of the door, but a germ of an idea came into her brain.

'Mr Truebury,' she said. 'You are very early. We do not usually receive callers until three in the afternoon.'

'I know, dear lady, but I had to see you.'

'Come into the drawing room, Mr Truebury,' said Patricia. She ushered him in and then closed the door in the butler's shocked face. Any unmarried lady when entertaining a gentleman should always leave the door open.

Mr Truebury suddenly felt nervous. Lord Charles had vowed to break his neck if he approached Miss Patterson again, which was why he had been lurking in the square in the hope of seeing Lord Charles leave. But what if he should return?

'I only called to beg you to consider my suit, Miss Patterson,' he said in a rush.

'I *might* consider your suit, Mr Truebury,' said Patricia slowly, 'if you could perform a small service for me.'

Hope rushed into Mr Truebury's heart as he saw all his duns melting away like the snow in spring.

'Anything,' he said fervently.

'I have had a certain falling out with my guardian and would like to get away by myself for a little. Do you know of any lady who might be glad of my company as a companion, say, for a few weeks?'

Money, or the hope of it, always made Mr Truebury's not normally strong brain work like lightning. 'There is my mother,' he said, promptly resurrecting that poor lady from her grave. 'She lives at our house in Richmond—a great barn of a place—and is cursed lonely. I could take you there.'

'I would be most grateful,' said Patricia. 'But I must ask you to curb your attentions to me, Mr Truebury, until I have quite made up my mind whether I want to marry or not.' She mentally added, 'The way I feel now, I would rather die an old maid.'

Mr Truebury thought rapidly. His father, Sir Egbert, was at Richmond and would see to it that Patricia was kept there under lock and key until she was forced to marry him.

'I have my carriage across the square,' he said hurriedly. 'We could leave immediately.'

'That will suit me very well,' Patricia said, to his infinite relief.

'Wait here and I will fetch some clothes.'

'I would rather wait across the square,' he said, looking about him nervously as if expecting Lord Charles to leap out from under a table.

'Then go,' said Patricia, 'but do not leave without me.'

'Wouldn't dream of it, dear lady,' said Mr Truebury, his hand on his heart. 'Wouldn't dream of it!'

EIGHT

The Lucases sat side by side on a sofa and looked sympathetically at their friend, Lord Charles Gaunt.

He talked about the weather, about the state of the nation, and about the war, all in equal tones of gloom.

'Dear Charles,' said Mrs Lucas at last. 'What really is the matter? I have never known you to look so worried *or* to be so *boring* before.'

Lord Charles gave them a rueful smile. 'The fact is, I am in a sad mess and I don't know what to do about it.'

Mrs Lucas got to her feet and poured him a glass of wine, and then said sympathetically, 'You will feel so much better if you tell us all about it. We are very good listeners, are we not, Mr Lucas? And sometimes if you talk out loud about what is bothering you, you often find the solution yourself.'

'It concerns Patricia,' said Lord Charles heavily.

'Ah, your pretty ward.'

'I wish to God I had never met her.'

'Dear me,' said Mrs Lucas. 'Well, you did, and you have, so you may as well begin at the beginning and tell us everything, or it is quite probable we will not know what you are talking about.'

So Lord Charles began to tell them of going to Burnham House to take up his duties as guardian, of Patricia's disgraceful behaviour with the soldier, of his discovery of her letter, and of his subsequent drunken near rape of her.

'And now I have broken off my engagement to Miss Chalmers,' ended Lord Charles, 'and it seems as if I am honour-bound to marry my ward after my behaviour.'

'What a perfectly splendid idea,' cried Mrs Lucas, clapping her hands.

'I say, steady on,' mumbled George Lucas, looking nervously at Lord Charles's set face.

'I don't see what's so splendid about getting married to a minx who only set out to make me fall in love with her.'

'She may have set out to do so,' said Mrs Lucas, 'but I do not believe that such a charming and pretty girl would go through with it. She was very, very young when you banished her to America, Charles. And you *did* go on like the wicked guardian. You know you did. You forced lessons on those sisters of yours, or tried to fill up their minds with heavy facts to improve *their* behaviour. I am sure she dreamed of revenge when she was in America but soon forgot about it when she saw you again. *You* are still in love with her, and that is a very rare and precious thing. And I will tell you another thing, I believe her to be in love with you. So there!'

'How on earth can she still love me after last night—if she ever did?'

'Of course she can. Love is not easily put off. Stop looking so gloomy, Charles. I shall put on my bonnet and go with you. She will listen to me.'

Lord Charles suddenly smiled. 'No, you terrifying woman, I can do my own courting.'

He was walking away from their house when he saw Mrs Grant with her daughters on the other side of the road. He was all at once anxious to make sure they would not broadcast any scandal about Patricia. He would call on Miss Sinclair later and make sure she had not said anything to Mary out of spite.

Mrs Grant was delighted to see him. She said they were staying with friends close by and invited him back with them to take tea. Lord Charles hated spending more time away from Patricia, but he realized he could hardly raise such a delicate subject in the middle of the pavement, and so he went with them.

After half an hour, he left with repeated assurances from all the Grants that that 'silly little scandal' had been completely forgotten.

Still, he hesitated. The temptation to tie up all the loose ends was very strong. He did not want to face his now ex-fiancée so soon. But after a short deliberation, he set out for the Chalmers' home. To his surprise, he met his secretary, who was just leaving.

'I have been arranging lodgings for Miss Sinclair,' said Mr Johnson stiffly. 'She is quite overset and very remorseful. She does not want to stay with the Chalmers because she feels they encouraged her to spy on Miss Patterson.'

'Still, I am desirous of seeing Miss Sinclair,' said Lord Charles. 'My ward was involved in a minor scandal before she went to America and I do not wish Miss Sinclair to tell anyone about it.'

'She would not. You have my word on it,' said Mr Johnson, colouring up.

'Indeed? And what makes you so sure?'

'Because I believe Miss Sinclair may shortly do me the honour of becoming my wife.'

'This is a surprise. Are you sure of your choice?'

'Very sure...with your permission, my lord, or without it.'

'Then I shall rely on you to see she keeps silent.'

After he had left Mr Johnson, Lord Charles hurried off in the direction of Cavendish Square.

He knew now that he loved Patricia as much as he had done when he had spoken to her at Lady Blessington's. He wanted to take her in his arms and kiss all the hurt and fright and worry from her face.

The first face that he saw on entering his home was full of hurt and fright and worry. But it was the face of Miss Simpkin.

'Patricia...*gone,*' she sobbed. 'All m-my f-fault.'

He felt fear clutch at his heart.

'What is all this?' he demanded sharply. 'Speak!'

'Not here,' whispered Miss Simpkin, looking nervously over her shoulder at the listening servants.

Lord Charles ushered the sobbing governess into the library. 'Now, hurry up. Out with it,' he commanded.

Miss Simpkin stopped sobbing and faced him bravely.

'I was a baker's daughter,' she said, 'but my mother had ideas above her station and had me educated like any fine lady. Sir Egbert Truebury came into the shop one day, and was much taken with me. I used to be quite pretty then,' she added wistfully.

She held up a hand as Lord Charles made an impatient gesture. 'You must bear with me, my lord, or you will not be able to understand my subsequent behaviour.

'My parents put silly ideas of marriage in my head and encouraged Sir Egbert to call. One day he asked if he could take me to a local fair, and my parents gave their consent. But he took me to his house instead, and...he constrained me to be his mistress. I was too ashamed to return home again. After a time, he tired of me but said he would set me up with my own seminary.

'For a while I was happy. I began to know what it was to be respected. Then one day Sir Egbert came back. He had several very noisy gentlemen with him. He demanded that I arrange tea parties during which his friends could meet the young ladies of the seminary. I refused. He said he would tell the whole town of my past and I would be ruined.

'I did not know what to do. He said he would return the following month for my answer. I sold the seminary very quickly, and sent Sir Egbert the money I had gained from the sale through a lawyer. I had immediately advertised in the newspapers for a position and was relieved when Mr and Mrs Patterson employed me.

'I was so happy with my dear Patricia. And then I met Sir Egbert that evening at Vauxhall. He said that unless I helped his son, Geoffrey, marry Patricia, he would tell you of my past.

'Today, I had just made up my mind not to do anything he wanted. I decided to tell you myself. But then I found Patricia had gone.'

'Where?'

'I do not know. The servants say Mr Truebury called this morning when I was out and Patricia saw him. I do not know why, because she dislikes him. Mr Truebury left on his own and it was shortly after that Patricia was seen to leave carrying a bandbox.'

'I know Truebury's lodgings,' said Lord Charles. He picked up his hat.

'Oh, let me go with you,' begged Miss Simpkin. 'I had no hand in her disappearance.'

'No, Miss Simpkin. Wait here. I can go faster alone. And Patricia may return in my absence. Did she leave any letter?'

Miss Simpkin sadly shook her head.

Lord Charles set off for Mr Truebury's lodgings. He was not very surprised at Miss Simpkin's sad story. It was a well-known fact that at least half the ladies' seminaries of England were run by cast-off mistresses.

But he was worried and frightened —frightened that he had driven Patricia to do something dangerous.

Mr Truebury had two servants at his lodgings, a footman who occasionally acted as butler and a valet. Both were unsavoury individuals and Mr Truebury had told them to say he and his father had left that very morning to go on the Grand Tour.

Which all went to show that Mr Truebury's brain could go so far and no further.

'On the *Grand Tour!*' exclaimed Lord Charles wrathfully. 'With Napoleon's troops all over Europe?'

The butler-footman took one look at Lord Charles's menacing face and tried to shut the door. He was an ex-boxer and put all his strength behind it.

Lord Charles crashed his shoulder against the door and sent it and the footman crashing back.

'Help, Jem,' cried the footman.

The valet came rushing out of an inner room wielding a cudgel. He swung it at Lord Charles, who dodged and brought his fist up to land on the valet's jaw with a satisfactory thump.

The ex-boxer struggled to his feet and grasped Lord Charles from behind in a crushing grip. Lord Charles heaved him over his head like a sack of coals and sent him crashing down the narrow corridor of Mr Truebury's lodgings.

Lord Charles seized the cudgel. The

valet was out cold, but the ex-boxer was sitting up, dizzily shaking his head.

'You,' said Lord Charles. 'What is your name?'

'Giles Marsham,' grunted the footman, feeling his head with a beefy hand.

'Well, Giles Marsham, either you tell me where your master is to be found or I shall spread your brains all around the place with this cudgel.'

'The Quality shouldn't go around like bruisers a-breakin' of people's heads,' said the footman sulkily. 'I'll lose my employ.'

Lord Charles hefted the cudgel in his hand.

'Or your life,' he said sweetly. 'Take your pick, Giles Marsham!'

Only determination not to cry in front of such an obnoxious toad as Geoffrey Truebury kept Patricia dry-eyed. She also reminded herself sternly that she ought to be grateful to Mr Truebury. For one thing, he had made no overtures to her but seemed content to sit well over on his side of the carriage, gazing at the scenery.

The English countryside was looking its best. Everything was coming to life under the warm sun. New leaves trembled on branches in the lightest of breezes and lambs scampered about the fields where the new grass rolled lazily under the sun, so green it was like the colour of Lord Charles's eyes.

Patricia tentatively touched her still-swollen lips. She had told him she loved him, but that had seemed to disgust him more than anything else.

She stared bleakly out of the window at the smiling countryside seeing only weeks and months and years of grief ahead. Love *was* a sickness. Why did she have to go and fall in love? She could have had a comfortable marriage and children and a home of her own without all this burning, aching yearning.

'Where did you say your mother lived?' she said, breaking the silence.

'Richmond,' replied Mr Truebury laconically, 'on the river. Vastly pretty place. Not the main family place. We've got estates in Sussex.'

'I hope Mrs Truebury will not be too put out by my unexpected arrival?'

'Oh, no, nothing ever disturbs her,' said Mr Truebury cheerfully, aware that he spoke the truth for nothing had disturbed his late mother since she was laid to rest some ten years before.

They stopped for refreshment at an inn and Patricia found herself becoming even more pleased with Mr Truebury's restrained behaviour. He said thoughtfully that he would send one of his grooms ahead with a message to let his mother know of their impending arrival.

Patricia hoped Mrs Truebury would prove to be amiable and undemanding so that she could find some peace and quiet to try to get over the worst of her grief.

As they continued on their journey, she said warmly to Mr Truebury, 'You are a thoughtful and considerate companion, sir, and I shall always be grateful to you.'

'Thank you,' said Mr Truebury, beaming at her. Coercion and threats were more his father's business. Mr Truebury thought his marriage to Patricia might be arranged amicably.

The carriage at last turned in through tall mossy gateposts and made its way up a weedy drive. Tall tangled woods blotted out the sun and cast a green gloom into the carriage. Patricia shivered. The estate looked sadly run down.

The house came into view, a Gothic folly, tall and turreted. The windows did not seem to have been cleaned in years and had a closed, blind look about them as they peered through their shrouds of ivy.

Patricia allowed herself to be helped down from the carriage and stood looking up at the forbidding exterior of the house. For one moment she thought it was deserted and that Mr Truebury was playing some trick on her, but to her relief the heavy oak door was opened by a butler and behind him stood an elderly gentleman, every bit as highly painted as Mr Truebury.

'I am Sir Egbert Truebury, Geoffrey's father,' said the elderly gentleman, walking forward and taking both Patricia's hands in a warm clasp. 'My son sent a messenger ahead to warn me of your arrival. A room has been prepared for you.'

'You are most kind, sir,' smiled Patricia, grateful that Sir Geoffrey seemed to be as uninquisitive as his son about the reason for her flight from her guardian. Geoffrey Truebury had seemed to accept that she had had some sort of falling out with Lord Charles without bothering to ask further questions about it.

'Come along then,' he said. 'Betts,' he said to his butler, 'take Miss Patterson to her room. Tea will be served in the drawing room in half an hour, Miss Patterson.'

'Thank you,' said Patricia. 'I am anxious to meet your wife.'

'Oh, ah, her...yes. Well, you'll see her soon enough.'

Patricia followed the butler up the stairs. The oaken staircase was intricately carved with heraldic beasts, and a stained glass window checkered the treads with oblongs of purple and scarlet.

A footman followed, carrying Patricia's bandbox.

The butler led the way along a corridor on the second landing and opened a door. The bedroom he ushered Patricia into was small and smelled of damp and disuse. But a fire had been lit in the hearth and cans of hot water and soap placed on the toilet table.

The butler bowed and left. The young footman, an unsavoury-looking youth, placed Patricia's bandbox on a table at the end of the bed and proceeded to open it.

'Leave that,' said Patricia, half amused, half alarmed. 'The housemaids will put away my clothes.'

'Don't have no housemaids,' said the

footman. 'Master don't like female servants.'

'Then leave it all the same. I prefer to unpack my clothes myself.'

The footman bowed and slouched out.

'What a peculiar household!' thought Patricia. 'Perhaps poor Mrs Truebury will be really pleased to have some female companionship.'

She hung away her scanty wardrobe, after selecting a primrose yellow silk gown to change into. She could feel black grief threatening to overcome her and resolutely kept herself busy, washing her face and hands, arranging her hair, and putting on the fresh gown to fill in the time before going downstairs.

When she opened her bedroom door she found to her surprise that the footman who had carried up her bandbox was stationed outside, leaning against the wall with his arms folded.

Not liking the expression on his face, which was an odd mixture of cunning and servility, Patricia said sharply, 'What are you doing here?'

'I was told to wait for you, miss,' he said, ducking his head, ''case you lost your way.'

Patricia followed him along the corridor

and down the stairs.

The house was very quiet and still. Dust motes swam lazily in the coloured shafts of light from the stained glass window which lit the staircase.

'It is like a house in one of those romances I used to read,' thought Patricia. 'What a strange brooding air of menace!'

She straightened her dress and nervously patted her hair before entering the drawing room, hoping that Mrs Truebury would not take her in dislike.

But only Sir Egbert and Geoffrey were in the room. They rose to their feet at her entrance.

'Where is Mrs Truebury?' she asked, looking about at the room which was crammed with heavy, ugly furniture.

'Resting, my dear. Mrs Truebury always sleeps very sound,' said Sir Egbert.

For some reason this remark of his father's seemed to strike young Geoffrey as being exquisitely funny.

'But to pass the time until Mrs Truebury is ready to receive you, Geoffrey here will take you to see the pride of our estate. We have a most elegant folly on a little island on our lake. This house belonged to my dear father,' said Sir Egbert, 'and he channelled water from the Thames to make an artificial lake. It will only take a little while and then you may return and take tea.'

Patricia eagerly agreed, anxious to escape from the heavy atmosphere of the house.

She followed Geoffrey out and along a straggling weedy path which led through the overgrown gardens and shaggy lawns at the back of the house until it ended at the edge of a lake.

There was a little island in the middle on which stood a mock Grecian temple, its slim white pillars gleaming in the late sun.

Geoffrey helped Patricia into a flat-bottomed boat moored to a rickety wooden jetty and then began to pole her across. He was not a very expert punter and several times Patricia clutched onto the side of the boat in alarm. 'I cannot swim, Mr Truebury,' she said.

'I didn't think you would be able to,' was all he said. 'Most females can't.'

There was a scraping sound as the boat landed on a small pebbled beach on the island.

Seen close to, the temple was a depressing place, the bottom of its pillars green with damp. Weeds had thrust their way up through the cracks in the broken wooden floor.

'Isn't it splendid?' cried Geoffrey. 'I always think it the most romantic of places. Do excuse me but a moment, Miss Patterson. I must make sure the boat is secure.'

Patricia nodded and sat down on a marble seat in the temple. She felt depressed and sad and very, very tired. As soon as she was presented to Mrs Truebury, she would beg to be allowed to retire.

She thought of Lord Charles and tears welled up in her eyes.

Then she heard Geoffrey Truebury calling her name.

She got up and walked listlessly down to the little crescent of pebbles where the boat had beached.

But the boat had gone, and with it Mr Truebury.

She heard him call again and saw him some yards away out on the lake in the boat.

'Will you marry me?' he called.

Patricia took a deep breath. Nothing, she realized, would ever make her want to marry any such man as Geoffrey Truebury.

Too tired and upset to be diplomatic, she called back, 'No, I am afraid I can't,' she shouted back.

'Then you can stay there until you come to your senses.' He grinned.

Patricia looked at him as if she could not believe her ears. 'Do not play silly games. Where is your mother? She will be upset and angry when she learns of your cruel jokes.'

'I told you, nothing upsets her,' said Geoffrey. 'She's been dead for ten years.'

'So *that* is why he was so eager to help me,' thought Patricia.

Then she remembered that Lord Charles's servants must have seen her leaving shortly after Mr Truebury's call.

'Lord Charles will find me,' she said.

'He won't know where to look,' laughed Geoffrey, his voice carrying clearly across the water. 'Papa won this awful old place at the card tables six months ago. Nobody knows we have it. Our family place is down in Sussex. Anyway, my servants have been told to tell Lord Charles that Papa and I have gone on the Grand Tour.'

'Don't be a fool,' snapped Patricia. 'He will never believe that such a worm as you would dare to venture abroad in the middle of a war.'

Geoffrey's mouth fell open in dismay. Then he rallied. 'Well, he won't come looking for you here. Papa and I will be in London tomorrow showing ourselves out and about, and if Lord Charles calls at our place in Sussex, it'll take him a long time to get here. Scream if you like. Nobody'll hear you. But there you stay until you've decided to marry me!'

He began to punt energetically and inexpertly toward the opposite shore.

'They cannot do this to me,' thought Patricia. 'It is all a bluff.'

But the sun was rapidly sinking and a chill wind was beginning to blow over the water.

Patricia began to panic. She was terrified at the thought of spending a night in the middle of an island surrounded by water.

If only she had learned to swim.

She stared furiously down at the greenish-brown water. It was so muddy she could not even see the bottom. *How* did one learn how to swim? Surely, by simply getting into the water and *trying*.

But if she found she could *not* learn, then she would have to spend a night on the island, soaking wet. Then she remembered she had a tinderbox in her reticule.

For a start, she would set the temple on fire so that even if no one from outside came to see what the matter was, at least she would be warm if she failed to learn how to swim.

She diligently went about the small island, picking up as many scraps of dry wood as she could find. She carried them all to the temple and heaped them up on the remains of the wooden floor. Lighting anything with a tinderbox took at least half an hour, and Patricia laboured with it, thinking she would never get the cotton waste to produce the necessary glow to ignite the timber. A violet dusk had settled over the surrounding countryside and an owl hooted mournfully from the woods on the far shore.

Then a little tongue of yellow flame licked its way up through the little pieces of tinder. Patricia retreated to safety as the flames burned higher until soon the whole wooden floor of the temple was blazing merrily.

'Now, I cannot waste time seeing if the fire will bring anyone,' she lectured herself severely. 'It is time for your first swimming lesson, Patricia Patterson!'

She walked down to the beach and placed her bonnet and reticule on a rock. She decided to keep on her shoes, which were little more than flat slippers, in case the rocks in the water were sharp. She tucked the skirt of her gown inside her drawers and tied them firmly by the tapes at her waist.

Then she gingerly walked into the water. It was ice-cold. She looked longingly back at the blazing fire. But no one had shouted or come running, and so she ploughed on until the water was up to her waist.

'Now,' she thought, 'you have watched the village boys. They kick out with their arms and legs and you will do the same. It is all very easy.'

She lifted her feet from the bottom and thrashed out wildly with her arms and legs until she was exhausted. She raised her head to see if she had moved at all and sank like a stone.

'Don't panic,' said a small voice of reason in her head. 'Don't panic or you will drown. Stand on the bottom and thrust yourself up to the air.'

Patricia thrust up, shot her head and shoulders up out of the water, and splashed down again. That was when she realized she could still stand on the bottom and keep her head above the water.

She stood up. The water was up to her neck. Behind her the burning temple sent a path of red light across the water. The other shore looked very far away.

Spreading her arms out on the water to maintain her balance, Patricia took a few tentative steps forward. The water still stayed just below her chin. She took a few more steps. Again, the water level did not rise.

Slowly, with increasing confidence, she made her way until she was past the halfway mark. It was then, as she ploughed on and the water level began to sink down below her shoulders that she realized that both Geoffrey and his father had been unaware of how shallow the lake was.

It was then that she knew that somehow she must make her way back to London. She would get as clear of the house as she could and then hope her clothes would dry as she walked. She would walk all night if need be.

Nothing mattered so long as she saw

Lord Charles again. He could curse her and shout at her and hate her, but he was her guardian, and she loved him, no matter what he did or said.

As she was making her way gingerly around the front of the house, she heard a great commotion.

'They must have spotted the fire,' she thought, shrinking back into the darkness of the shrubbery.

It was a moonless night so Patricia decided to move slowly to the front of the house, keeping always in the shadow of the bushes, and then make her way down the drive and out into the road.

She tried not to hurry, although she was shivering with cold and the desire for freedom was great.

The front of the house came into view. Keeping a wary eye on it in case anyone looked out of the window, Patricia headed for the drive.

A great splintering of glass and a scream made her whip around. A figure came flying through a downstairs window, thrown straight through the glass, and landed in an inert heap on the lawn.

The row from the house was tremendous. Then there was a shot and silence. The figure on the lawn groaned and then lay still.

Shaking with fear, she crept forward and looked down. In the light of the stars, the unconscious face of the Truebury footman looked up at her.

And then clear as a bell, a familiar and beloved voice shouted, 'Where is she? Answer me, Truebury, or I will blow your horrible head from your shoulders.'

NINE

'Charles!' screamed Patricia.

The footman's body had been thrown through the drawing room window.

Patricia ran headlong into the house, wrenched open the door of the drawing room, and stood like an apparition on the threshold.

She was as white as a sheet, and dripping wet. Bits of water weed clung to her gown and hair.

Lord Charles was standing by the fireplace, blood running from a cut at his mouth. Sir Egbert was crouched in an armchair, his old painted face a mask of hate. The butler was lying with his head in the coal scuttle and another footman lay stretched out on the hearth rug at his lordship's feet.

Geoffrey Truebury was clutching his wrist. 'You've broken it,' he was whining.

'Then that will teach you to try and put a bullet through me,' Lord Charles was saying as he looked up and saw Patricia.

For one dreadful moment, he thought she was dead and he was seeing her ghost.

Patricia would have run to him, but he said sharply, 'Don't come between me and them, Patricia. Stay where you are.'

He turned to Sir Egbert. 'I am taking my ward away from here. I shall find out the full story from her of what has happened. I do not want any scandal, which is why I have decided not to kill you—that is, unless I return in the next few days and find you still here, or, in fact, if I find you anywhere in England.'

He backed toward the door, holding the pistol very steady.

'She came of her own free will,' growled Sir Egbert. 'That's what you get by having your ward educated by that whore, Simpkin.'

'You do not have any hold over poor Miss Simpkin any more, Truebury,' said Lord Charles. 'She told me the whole nasty, sorry story. But I think I will take her something to remember you by.' He walked back and twitched the large diamond pin from Sir Egbert's stock.

'Come, Patricia,' said Lord Charles, his voice harsh with worry. 'If either of these monsters has tried to deflower you, I will shoot them on the spot.'

'No,' said Patricia, swaying against him. 'They put me on an island in the lake and said they would leave me there until I decided to marry Geoffrey Truebury.'

'Then let us go.'

Patricia shivered, her teeth chattering. 'My clothes are upstairs.'

'Then go and fetch them. I will wait here.'

Patricia ran all the way, weak as she was, frightened that some monster footman would leap out of a closet and attack her. She bundled her clothes back into the bandbox and dragged it back downstairs as fast as she could.

'Do you not have your carriage with you?' asked Patricia as they walked down the drive.

'It's at the gates. I knew if they had you here, they would hide you if they heard my arrival. But I do not have any servants with me. I was anxious to avoid scandal.'

'I don't care.' Patricia shivered. 'I cannot believe I am safe. They may come after us.'

'Nonsense. They would not dare.'

'I must tell you what happened...how I

236

came to be so silly,' panted Patricia, trying to keep up with his long strides.

He stopped and looked down at her, his eyes glinting in the starlight. 'My love,' he said softly, 'you can tell me everything over the nearest, hottest supper.'

The table cover had been removed and bowls of fresh fruit and nuts studied their reflections in the polished mahogany of the dining table. Patricia and Lord Charles had dined at The Star and Garter in Richmond after Patricia had been fussed over by the maidservants, who had been told miss had been attacked by vicious footpads while out walking and thrown in the Thames.

'Now, Patricia,' said Lord Charles, 'the servants have retired and left us alone at last. What happened? Why did you let a monster like Truebury take you away? I can hardly believe he dragged you off.'

'When I knew you were disgusted with me,' said Patricia, 'I could not bear to stay in your house any longer. Mr Truebury called by chance. He seemed harmless if obnoxious—too weak to be a real villain. I asked him if he knew of any lady who might be glad to have me as a companion for a few weeks. He said his mother

237

lived at Richmond and would be glad to entertain me.

'Oh, it all seemed so innocent. I packed a bandbox and met him in his carriage at the far side of the square. He behaved very well on the journey. I felt uneasy when I arrived at the house because of the atmosphere. And there were no female servants. Mr Truebury, the son, said he would row me out to an island to see a folly. When we were there, he said he was going to make sure the boat was securely tied, but when I went to look for him, he had pushed off. He said I might stay there until I promised to marry him. He must be desperate for money.'

'His father has plenty,' said Lord Charles dryly, 'but he is a skinflint and, I believe, had told Geoffrey he would no longer meet his gambling debts and suggested marriage to you as a means of his son's gaining money.'

'Oh. Well, I was frightened and I cannot swim. Like a fool I told Geoffrey that. I set fire to the temple—'

'You did *what?*'

'I set fire to the temple, and a fat lot of good it turned out to be since even you did not notice the blaze.'

'I was only determined to save you. I looked neither to right nor left.'

'In any case,' went on Patricia, 'I also thought if I found I could not learn to swim, I could return to the fire and dry my clothes. Swimming appears to be a very hard thing to master with one lesson and I thought I would drown. But Geoffrey did not know—and I found out—that the water is not very deep and I was able to wade across.

'I was about to make my way down the drive to safety when the footman came flying through the window and I heard your voice.'

'I thought you were a ghost when I saw you standing there,' said Lord Charles.

'Were you much hurt?' asked Patricia.

'Not very. The footman managed to land a good punch before I threw him out. Then Geoffrey dragged out a pistol and tried to shoot me. I do hope I did break his wrist.'

A silence fell between them. Their private dining room overlooked the Thames. Water chuckled beneath the windows.

'The...the revenge, Lord Charles,' ventured Patricia at last. 'It was part of my childhood, part of a fantasy. All the time I was in Boston, you were The Wicked Guardian out of a Gothic novel.'

'I understand,' he said gently. 'I bitterly regret my own behaviour, for it means we *must* marry.'

'I don't want to must marry,' wailed Patricia tearfully and ungrammatically. 'No one knows what really happened. I could say you came to my bedroom to give me a lecture. I don't want to *have* to marry you.'

Patricia rose, knocking back her chair, and fled from the room.

Lord Charles cursed fluently under his breath. He should have waited until she had had a good night's sleep and then put the matter to her reasonably and sensibly.

He rose and went to her bedroom, but the room was empty. Suddenly frightened, he ran down the stairs and out of the inn. It was very dark, but he could see the glimmer of the pale green gown she had worn at dinner a little way along the path by the river.

He walked toward her as quietly as possible, wondering desperately what to say. If marriage to him was so abhorrent, then he would need to let her go. His side hurt where the butler had punched him. He felt battered and bruised and infinitely weary.

He came up behind her and put his hands on her shoulders. She trembled and leaned back against him and closed her eyes.

'Patricia,' he said softly, 'you do not need to marry me. I will do what I can to make sure there is not any scandal. Please do not be upset. You have been through a dreadful experience. Return with me now and go to bed. Everything will seem better in the morning.'

Patricia turned and faced him. She seemed to be summoning up the last of her courage. 'Then kiss me good night,' she said, her voice barely above a whisper.

'If we are not to be wed, then I should not kiss you,' he said sadly.

'A guardian may kiss his ward.'

He tilted up her chin and kissed her very gently on the lips. He made to draw away, but she wound her arms tightly about him and buried her fingers in the thick hair above his collar.

'Patricia,' he said with a mixture of gladness and wonder in his voice. 'Oh, Patricia.' He kissed her savagely and passionately and then gave her a little shake.

'And *that*, Miss Patricia Patterson,' he said, 'is why we must marry.'

'Charles, do you love me?'

'With all my heart.'

'I love you so terribly, Charles. When I thought you hated me, I was sure my heart would break.'

'Then we had better be married as soon as possible, before I do any more of this...and this...and this...'

They returned to London on the following day, having agreed to be married in a month's time.

Miss Simpkin was in a twittering state of apprehension when they arrived back from Richmond. She had been waiting hourly in a strung-up nervous condition, dreading to learn that some horrible fate had befallen Patricia, dreading to hear of her own dismissal. She burst into noisy tears of relief on seeing her beloved Patricia and then cried again when Lord Charles invited her to the wedding.

He presented her with the diamond pin he had taken from Sir Egbert, remarking dryly that he was sure Sir Egbert had meant to give her a present all along.

It seemed to Patricia as if she immediately plunged into a hectic round of shopping and arrangements. In the days following the announcement of the wedding a few carping members of society spoke darkly about the sinister haste of the marriage, but the rest vied eagerly for invitations.

Patricia and Lord Charles had decided to spend a lengthy honeymoon in Boston. Their trunks had to be packed and sent on ahead to the ship at Bristol, and so, a week before the wedding, Patricia, aided by Miss Simpkin, was trying to decided which clothes she should pack.

'Oh, do take this pretty muslin,' said Miss Simpkin, holding up a dainty white gown. 'It is monstrous exciting the way everything has worked out for the best—although it does distress me that you, dear Patricia, found out that I was a Fallen Woman.'

'A most unfortunate lady, *not* a fallen woman,' said Patricia gently. 'I told you how very ruthless both Sir Egbert and his son were. They will not trouble you again. People can be very cruel and it is all too easy for an unfortunate woman to lose her reputation. Some are even hinting that Lord Charles was *forced* to marry me because we spent the night at the inn at Richmond. We could not tell anyone *why* we were both in Richmond because Lord Charles said he did not want any gossip or scandal or court cases. It appears the Trueburys have left the country, but still, the whispers and rumours *do* hurt.'

'It is only the jealous ones who have not been invited to the wedding who complain,' said Miss Simpkin, 'and no one listens to them. Also, it might have come out, were there an investigation, that you went willingly with Mr Truebury. It is better this way.'

Patricia laughed. 'You sound just like Nanny Evans—"Lord Charles knows best." '

'Well, it appears he does, my love,' said Miss Simpkin. 'Such generosity and understanding! I was so sure I would be turned off without a character.'

Nanny Evans had arrived, prepared to enjoy the wedding, but fully expecting to accompany Patricia on the honeymoon as well. When she was not asleep which was fortunately often, she followed Patricia about, convinced the young girl she had nursed was still in need of constant care.

'Oh, Simpers,' sighed Patricia. 'I will

be so glad when I can be alone with my husband. No, I do not mean I want to get rid of *you*, it is just that this house always seems to be bulging at the seams with members of the ton, hell-bent on getting an invitation to the wedding. We only planned to invite a few people, Lord Charles's sisters and people like that, but everyone keeps calling, bearing *such* expensive gifts that we do not have the heart to tell them they cannot come.'

'Including that creature Sinclair,' sniffed Miss Simpkin. 'What a horror *she* turned out to be.'

'Miss Sinclair was misled, that is all. She is to marry Mr Johnson, as you know, and he is an estimable man.'

'Indeed,' said the little governess crossly. 'It appears the wicked do flourish like the green bay tree.'

'I draw the line at inviting Miss Chalmers,' said Patricia. 'I never want to see that woman again.'

'I doubt if Lord Charles wants to see her again either,' said Miss Simpkin, 'and that is all that matters. Rumour has it Miss Chalmers is already being courted by some gentleman of the church, although I have not yet learned his name.'

'They will probably suit each other very well,' said Patricia tartly. 'They can both sit and moralize and preach and make everyone quite miserable. I cannot quite hate Miss Chalmers as much as I feel I should. I am so very lucky, it makes me wish well of the whole world—or nearly the whole world,' she added, thinking of the Trueburys. 'When I think I nearly ruined my reputation irrevocably with that drunken young captain. I wonder what became of him.'

'My dear! The strangest thing. I had quite forgot to tell you,' said Miss Simpkin. 'He called the day you disappeared and I was so overset I could hardly listen to what he was saying. I saw him alone—at least I had enough wit for *that*. I was so afraid he meant to make trouble.'

'And did he...want to make trouble?' asked Patricia nervously.

'Not a bit of it. He was back on leave from the wars and he called to say how sorry he was about that awful business and how it had been on his conscience. It turned out his commanding officer knew he was the culprit but did not want to lose a good soldier. I am afraid the poor captain got hundreds of lashes and nearly died anyway. He left this letter for you. I still have it in my reticule,' said Miss Simpkin, scrabbling about in a large droopy velvet sack.

Patricia took the letter from her and tore it up into little pieces.

'But why did you not read it?' exclaimed Miss Simpkin. 'I am sure it it was vastly romantic.'

'And I am equally sure Lord Charles would be furious if he found it. No, Simpers, some things are better left unread.'

'Patricia!'

Lord Charles appeared in the doorway.

'I wish to have a word with you in private.'

Patricia rose to her feet, and Miss Simpkin prepared to accompany her.

'No, Miss Simpkin,' said Lord Charles. 'We have been faithfully chaperoned by you since our return, but what I have to say to Patricia is for her ears alone.'

'Is anything the matter?' asked Patricia, looking anxiously up into his set face.

'Yes,' he said curtly. 'Come along.'

Patricia walked nervously with him out of the room, a lump like ice in her stomach. 'He has decided he does not love me,' she thought. He led the way downstairs, calling over his shoulder to the butler who was standing in the hall, 'We shall be in the library. See we are not disturbed.'

He held open the door for Patricia, followed her into the room, and turning, locked the door.

'Oh, what is wrong, Charles?' cried Patricia. 'You look so angry and stern.'

He walked over to the fireplace and put one booted foot on the fender, leaned his arm on the mantel, and looked down into the flames of the small fire that was burning on the hearth.

'Since our return from Richmond, Patricia,' he said heavily, 'I have not been alone with you once. I have observed the conventions very strictly.'

'Yes, Charles,' whispered Patricia.

'Every time I return to this house, my drawing room seems to be full of posturing jackanapes paying court to you.'

'Only members of the ton anxious to secure an invitation to the wedding,' said Patricia. 'We are all the crack.'

'And does that matter so much to you?' he asked huskily.

'The only thing that matters, Charles,'

said Patricia with a catch in her voice, 'is you. I cannot bear to think you might not love me.'

He turned to face her and held out his arms. 'That, my little love,' he said softly, 'is my fear too.'

'Oh, *Charles*,' cried Patricia, running into his arms. 'Kiss me. I am so weary of being conventional.'

He caught her to him and kissed her fiercely and passionately and then long and languorously until he felt her tremble in his arms.

He put her away from him and said shakily, 'Soon I will have you in my bed and in my arms and all these noisy chattering people will not be able to plague us or make me worry about our love. Oh, Patricia, my only love.'

'Your *only* love? You keep a miniature of a vastly beautiful woman beside your bed, as I recall.'

'Not content with putting stuffed hedgehogs in my bed, you also pried into my love life. No, my love, that is a miniature of my mother.'

Patricia gave a happy little sigh and raised her lips to his.

'No, Patricia, do not kiss me again. I

can barely wait for our wedding as it is.'

She pressed her body against his and wound her fingers in the thick hair which curled over his collar at the back of his neck.

He lifted her up in his arms, his green eyes glinting down at her flushed face and the swell of her bosom.

'My sweeting,' he said, tightening his arms about her. 'You seem determined to turn me into a wicked guardian after all!'